The High Arc Vampires

Revitalized

JESSICA CAGE

Jamie,

With every bit
of magic, there may
be major consequences.
Enjoy the story!
-xoxo-

JCage
8-26-2020

REVITALIZED

JESSICA CAGE

Cover design by Cover It Designs

Book design by Jessica Cage

Printed in the United States of America

First Printing: January 2011

ISBN-13 978-1479200436

REVITALIZED

A note from the Author:

A special thanks to everyone who helped me get this out into the world. My talented baby brother who designed my 1st and 2nd covers for Revitalized and was completely understanding when I chose to go a new route with the 3rd, my understanding and encouraging mother who helped take care of Ameer while I worked. To all the reviewers I found help through on Facebook and Twitter, and my amazing editor who helped to clean up all the things I missed.

*To find out when more to the story will be
published, follow Jessica's Website at:*

www.jessicacage.com

This Book is dedicated to my bundle of Joy Ameer. You are my inspiration and my motivation, and I hope I can make you happy as well as proud.
I love you baby boy.
-Mommy

...it will heal your body and give you the life you deserve. The life you were always meant to have.

REVITALIZED

The ear piercing shrill of the clock radio alarm tore through my subconscious; crudely announcing that it was time to get up and face the day. It was just another day, nothing more; this was how I had to approach life. The pain I faced was too great to imagine years, months, weeks, or even more days ahead of the moment I was currently in. Each morning was tainted with the fear that I would fall to my knees and break as soon as my feet landed on the cold wooden floor that surrounded my bed, and this morning was no different.

My frizzy, auburn hair surrounded my face partially covering my eyes. The sunlight passing through the strands lit them up and reminded me of flames. For a moment, I wondered what it would feel like if the coarse locks had suddenly ignited and

1

engulfed me in the blaze. Sure, it would be painful, but how would it compare to the pain that was already there? I flicked the hair away with one hand, and blew away the strands that were stuck to my lips.

The ceiling above my bed usually worked as a focal point when my mind started to wander. The patterns created by the cracks in the crème colored paint, were passages for lost thoughts. Every morning was the same; I woke up to the harsh reminder of what my life had become. One unfortunate scratch on the painting of my existence had grown out of control, and branched out into a million tiny cuts; each going in their own direction birthing more fissures until I could barely recognize what I was looking at. The image had become so distorted that it pained me to think of it.

The condition of the ceiling testified to the amount of neglect my home had taken since it been placed in my care. The house needed a lot of work; nothing too major, mainly cosmetic touch ups here and there. It needed a new coat of paint inside and out. I couldn't say that I was completely sure I would've made the changes if I were physically able. Someone could have been brought in and paid to make the improvements for me, but this house, with its chipped paint, cracked walls, and rusted hinges was my only comfort. It was all I had left to remind me of a time before pain, before everything went wrong. I'm not saying there was any sound logic to my thinking, but there was a sense of comfort in it.

REVITALIZED

This place was the backdrop to my happy childhood. I was an only child, and was happy, and surrounded by love and complete acceptance and understanding. My parents let me be myself and never questioned me for it. Even when I doubted myself, they were supportive. When I experimented with my appearance or altered my interests, they welcomed changes with open arms. I cringed as the memory of their smiling faces fixated in front of my eyes for a second before they transformed into two cold boxes. It was time to get up.

I took a deep breath silently preparing myself and building up the courage to face the day. I gripped the edge of the covers and tossed them aside. I swung my legs over the edge of the bed and my feet landed on the cool hardwood floor. It was a product of design that my slippers were clear across the room. The shock of the chill was good for me; it sent an icy wave through my legs that up the rest of my reluctant body. My limbs shivered as I quickly tiptoed across the floor to my slippers. They were my favorite pair; big, floppy, puppy faces that felt like warm clouds hugging my feet.

After putting on my slippers, I headed downstairs to begin my usual morning routine. To stop myself from thinking of all the repairs that needed to be done, I tried to focus more on how beautiful the house was despite the obvious flaws. I stopped on the steps, gripping the railing that reminded me so much of my father. He'd put his entire heart into every crevice of our

3

home. Not unlike my mother, he was a stickler for details, something I had always considered to be interesting. They were both so particular, but it never seemed to cause an issue. Their eccentricities were the same. I closed my eyes as his smile flashed through my mind, and I held it there for as long as I could. It was getting harder to remember him, harder to bring his face into focus.

He chose this house for us, small and quaint, nothing too flashy, though he could have afforded more. A successful investor and real estate agent, my father had done well for himself. Despite that, he felt it was necessary for me to live an average life, which would have been impossible if I lived in a world where everything came too easily. He wanted us to build a home, and shape it into what we wanted. He wanted me to know what it meant to take an idea and mold it until the dream became reality. The very mention of hiring a professional to touch up the place always made him shiver. He couldn't stand the idea of some stranger tainting our home. We moved here when I was five, and I was encouraged to help with every decision, though I honestly had no real input. I just picked the prettiest colors, which is why my room looked like a disfigured rainbow until I was 16.

My fingers dug into the grooves along the railing. My father was a talented craftsman. It took him nearly two months to finish it. I remembered it vividly; every night after dinner, he would carve away at the mahogany banister creating the intricate design, while my mother and I sat at the top of the stairs and watched as closely as we could without disturbing him. He took pleasure in his work, and he used to hum, 'Whistle While You Work' under his breath. The tune rang in my ears as if he was still there, humming in his own offbeat melody. He enjoyed it so much that over time, the carvings appeared in every room of the house. For years, I would find him intently working on the designs and mumbling about making them perfect. It was a better vice than alcohol or smoking.

The wall lining the staircase was littered with picture frames. This was my mother's project, something she took pride in that I now thanked her for. She was the embodiment of what one would call a shutterbug; snapping pictures at every event, no matter how unimportant others thought they were. I stopped and stared at a picture of her and my father laughing. Her head lay on his shoulder and her arms were wrapped tightly around him. Hanging in a faded gold frame, it was the first picture put on that wall and was still my favorite. They were much younger then and were illuminated with a brilliant light that I loved to imagine originated from their inner happiness.

I found myself lost in concentration, matching her features to my own, picking apart her face as I always did when I stopped at this picture. Her eyes were my eyes; light brown, almost hazel, and when the sun hit them, it highlighted the subtle hints of green. We shared the same honey brown skin, though hers was clear and even, while mine was now blotchy and dry; a side effect of the medication. If she were still here, she would freak out to see how just how little effort I'd given to taking care of myself. I continued to go over my features in my head, matching their faces to mine. I had my father's thin nose and lips, combined with my mother's pout and a mixture of both of their smiles. (You could see it when I had a reason to smile, which was something that hadn't happened in a long time.)

As I made it to the kitchen, I was greeted by the red light blinking on the answering machine. The notification gave no pause for thrill or concern, because it was the same person every day. She left the same message asking me to call her. She was my last living relative, being the only child of two only children; my maternal grandmother, who believed she had a way to heal me that no doctor would ever dream of, because it would put him "right out of business." She was old, wise, stubborn in her ways, and held on tightly to what my mother called 'dark magic'. Whenever my mother referred to her practices as such, my grandmother simply waved her off. She wasn't the type to force anyone into accepting her beliefs. She'd always said that if a person didn't truly believe in its power, it would chew them up and spit them out. She was however, livid with my mother for forcing her views onto me. She wanted me to come to my own conclusions about magic just as she had given my mother the freedom to do.

REVITALIZED

It was often that I overheard the discussions they had about me and how important it was that I knew where I came from. My grandmother referred to me as 'a natural' and my mother hissed ugly curses at her every time she did. This was always followed by my grandmother kissing me on the forehead and floating out the door wearing a carefree smile; while my mother stormed up the stairs to her bedroom, slamming the door as if she was a schoolgirl who had just been punished for breaking curfew. I would be lying if I said I didn't enjoy their confrontations, I mean what girl wouldn't enjoy seeing their mom basically being sent to her room. It was pure entertainment!

I wished I could believe in my grandmother's 'dark magic', and her 'cure'. From time to time, I let myself drift into fantasies that it could be real. I'd be able to go back to living my life, the life I loved, and the life that was taken away. I pictured the friends I had alienated to prevent tainting their lives with my pain. I thought of the sports and activities that once filled my life and how strong I was, but now to even try and perform one tenth of the physical activity that I once enjoyed, would probably cause my sickly body to shatter.

I heard my mother's voice clearly, "That woman and her superstitious ways. You will not take part in any of that. It isn't natural!" My mother would never approve of my grandmother's alternative healing methods. She tried her hardest to keep us apart in fear that I would somehow fall for her words and follow her way of thinking. I never understood why this would be so horrible. Was she afraid that I would be closer to my grandmother than I was to her? What was the big deal? What harm could possible come from building that relationship?

After years of these and many questions like them going unanswered I stopped asking. Any effort to try and sneak behind my mother's back to visit my grandmother was useless. No matter how duplicitous I could be my mother always knew, though it was much easier to trick my father. Maybe she was using a little 'black magic' of her own. She would never admit if she were.

After a while, I stopped sneaking to see my grandmother. Partially because of my mother's judgmental tone, and partially because my schedule had become so jammed with social events after I started junior year in high school, but mostly because I started to feel strange whenever I was around her. It was like there was something buried inside of me that I could only feel when I was with her. Whatever it was, it had been stirring, waking, and sometimes felt as if it were clawing to get out. With each visit, the feeling only intensified. She never said anything about it, and I never mentioned it, but she seemed to be aware of what was happening with me. I forced myself to ignore it. Stifled, the feeling went away, and I never thought about it again.

REVITALIZED

I put off the message and headed to the counter where a total of eight pills waited in the daily compartment of my weekly pillbox. I frowned at the idea of forcing them down my throat, because I had never acquired a tolerance for them. One pill always led to the next. Each one fixed one issue and caused another. I argued with my mother that I'd be better off without them, and she told me I had no idea what I was talking about. I longed for my mothers' warm arms around me and her soft voice whispering in my ear that it would all be okay. It felt like only days ago she had been here with me, helping me through it all. I shook the thought from my mind, got a glass of water, and swallowed each pill down as quickly as I could while ignoring the pain as each one punctured a new hole in my throat, leaving its bitter signature on the way down.

It'd been two years spent in this monotonous morning routine, and one year since I'd been doing it alone. It was one of the few things that felt dependable. Standing in the large open concept kitchen, everything was always where it was expected it to be. I made sure to keep it that way; one of the few things my mother was adamant about. Her kitchen had to be in top condition. Everything was assigned a designated place and position. 'Labels forward Alexa, always forward!' There was a time when the thought of coming anywhere near this room was dreaded. Not wanting to hear her scrutiny when a cup didn't make it back to its rightful cabinet, or if a fork landed in the section of the utensil drawer that was meant for spoons. Sometimes just for fun, I would move things around so that I could time her and see how long it would take until she had put them all back in order. Once the room I avoided against all odds, this was where I spent most of my time now. It was where I felt the safest and the closest to her.

Something about the room made my mom feel more at ease, this was her sanctuary. Every morning she made sure there was hot breakfast for my father and I, never forgetting to remind us that cold cereal was no way to start the day. I stopped at the refrigerator door, remembering the smell of her pancakes. The ones with the secret ingredient she never got to tell me about. She promised to give it to me, along with all of her other special recipes, on my 21st birthday. It would have been the start of a new tradition, something for me to pass on to my children. My heart ached as I realized I would never be able to taste them again. I tried to remember it. I tried to focus on the flavor in my mouth, the smell was strong, but the taste was spoiled by the pills I'd just taken. I gave up and went on with my routine.

I retrieved the bowl of fruit I'd cut up before I went to bed the night before, and a bottle of orange juice, grabbed a fork from the drawer and started to eat while still standing at the counter. I couldn't sit at the table anymore. It flooded my head with memories of all the meals I had there with them. The laughter that erupted as my dad told me embarrassing details about my mom when they were younger. I remembered trying to hide the blood that rushed to my cheeks as they attempted to have the drug talk and even worse when they brought up the boy talk. I hadn't built up enough courage to sit there, but I could never get rid of it. So, I stared at it from a distance, making sure to never make contact with it. Even after a year, the resistance to it had not faltered.

The round mahogany table, with its four matching chairs, taunted me in what became a childish voice in my head. The designs carved into their legs and on the center of the table were similar to the ones in the banister. The dust that settled on its top was thick enough to be mistaken for a tablecloth. I could barely make out the color of the wood under the gray film. I hadn't touched it at all since that night. My grandmother's worried eyes, I could see them. She was there with me, I'm not sure how she knew, but, she was there before the police even showed up. I was grateful for her presence, for her arms wrapped around me and her shoulder to cry on.

I treaded heavily over to the phone and watched the blinking light on the answering machine. It would be her. No one else called me anymore. At first it felt like they were giving me space, the distance I had asked for, but eventually like most thing that go unseen, I had been forgotten, except for her. She called every day and her voice on that machine had also become a part of my daily routine.

As I pressed the playback button I popped a chunk of cantaloupe in my mouth and damn near choked when I heard the voice.

"Hey girl, it's me…Jazz. I know we haven't spoken in a while, but hell, you are still my sister and I miss you…call me." The sound of my once best friend's voice echoed throughout the room as I pictured how she looked nearly a year ago when I last saw her. Her real name was, Jasmine, but she refused to be called that, declaring it to be too oppressive. I never understood that, but I accepted it anyway, not that she would have given me any other choice. I asked her once why she didn't just change it, and she said she wouldn't because she was named after her grandmother and didn't want to hurt her mother's feelings.

I could see her caramel skin, her almond shaped eyes, and the bouncy brown curls that surrounded her face. Her lips were full, almost overwhelming and smiling, like they always were. We had been friends since kindergarten; glued together at the hip. My mother loved it; she considered her a second daughter. We did just about everything together, except sports. She was more of a stereotypical girl and I was a natural born tomboy. She came to every event and every game to show her support and cheer me on, just as I did at every one of her fashion shows, because that's what friends do for each other.

She was an amazing designer, and even though she begged me to be in her shows, I never would. My body would not do justice to her wonderful designs. I thought of the dress she created for me for our senior prom. The one I never got to wear. It still hung in the back of my closet untouched. She had given it to me as a surprise only days before I got the news that flipped my world upside down. The pain had hit me so hard and without so much as a notification of what was to come. I missed the last few weeks of senior year. I graduated, but I never got to walk across the stage.

I remember the doctor's eyes, as he told me that I had Advanced Multiple Sclerosis. It was a disease that was now attacking my nervous system and causing me unbearable pain. After weeks of testing and physical therapy, I was put on medication. The doctor said it was an extreme case. I overheard him telling my mother, that at the rate of my progression, I only had months left before I wouldn't be able to get out of bed. He had never seen a case appear so suddenly and in such an advanced stage as mine. He wanted to enter me into a case study which my mother refused.

He was unable to explain how the disease had gone undiscovered, or the fast rate of the deceleration of my motor skills. There were no warning signs; no flashing red lights telling me to proceed with caution. I was at a track meet, the last one of my high school career. I took off running ahead of everyone else, on top of the world. My mother was in the crowd screaming with Jazz by her side cheering me on. My dad was filming from the top of the bleachers because he said it gave him a better shot. I was a few steps away from the finish when a final rush of adrenaline pumped through my veins. I was ecstatic, I was in the zone and I was winning. Seconds after I broke through the yellow tape, I hit the ground. My body writhing in pain, the adrenaline burned off and left behind a flame that seared through my muscles. In an instant I gone from running the fastest I had ever run, to facing the idea of never being able to walk again.

My mother refused the doctor's diagnosis, quit her part-time position at the local daycare, and every day forced me to fight through it. I never hated her for it, even though I wanted to give up so many times. She pushed me, not for herself, but for me. She wanted me to be strong and prove to myself that I was worth fighting for. That was when the barrier was really put up between me and my grandmother. She called every day begging my mother to let her help and of course was refused. I often overheard my mother arguing with my father who argued against her, though not nearly as forcefully as he could have.

"It couldn't hurt. Why not just try it? If it helps and takes away her pain, even a little bit, isn't that worth trying?" My father tried to talk some sense into my mother, but she simply would not hear it. He would look at me with such guilt in his eyes. As if he blamed himself for what was happening to me, I guess that is how any parent would feel, as though their own genetics had damned their child.

My mother felt my father would betray her and refused to let my grandmother be with me without 'proper supervision', which meant my mother hovering over us whenever she came to visit, even if my father was there. She couldn't allow my grandmother sneaking behind her back to try and taint me, as if she were going to poison my soul. She wouldn't even let me drink the store-bought tea she would bring for me, afraid she had found a way to slip something past the sealed cap!

I thought of my grandmother again. She hadn't called today like she always did. Was something wrong? I picked up the phone clumsily, nearly dropping it and dialed her number. The phone rang; each ring longer than the one before it. She wasn't home? She had no answering machine, so I couldn't leave her a message. The phone just kept ringing. I slammed the receiver down in the cradle and tried not to worry as I stuffed the remainder of the fruit down my throat, and tossed the dishes in the sink. Any other day I would wash them and put them back in their designated spot the way my mother would have, but, I was too distracted to care.

REVITALIZED

You may be wondering why I was so upset over one missed call, what is the big deal? After living inside of what was basically a controlled environment for so long, where everything is predictable, I was pretty much like a common test animal in a lab. Change one factor of their ecosystem and their little minds go ape shit.

Something inside me told me I needed to go and make sure that she was alright. I threw my clothes on hastily, oversized jeans and an orange t-shirt, (fashion icon over here) and moved as quickly as I could to get to my car in the garage. I tried to imagine that the phone had simply come unplugged, or she was out tending to her garden. I got to my car; the one my father had gotten me for my 16th birthday, a blue 2003 Chevy Malibu. Like the house and myself, it too had been poorly cared for. It was near the point where I would soon have to consider getting a new car, but it was hard to see the point in that since I rarely put it to use, and didn't know how much longer I would be able to drive at all.

I drove the 20-minute trip in ten and was shocked that I hadn't been pulled over; suburban police are usually on the lookout for early morning procrastinators speeding to get to work on time. I glanced around the front of my grandmother's overly accessorized front yard as I pulled to a stop; my heart ached when I didn't see her out there. I parked and once again forced my body to move as fast as it would toward her door. I told myself that I wouldn't regret it later, but knew that I would. Denial only gets you so far.

Stiff legs carried me up the stairs to the door, passing the whimsical garden gnomes, plastic swans, and the wildflowers that traced the fence outlining her property. Her house stuck out like a sore thumb on the street, one that I'm sure her neighbors were just thrilled about! It looked more like a cottage from a fairy tale than a suburban home. The wind blew, shaking the chimes that lined the porch. There was something dreamlike about this place that always led me to question the validity of my mother's concerns. I suddenly wished I had taken the time to figure out if there was anything to it.

As I pulled the spare key out of my bag, my fingers began to cramp; it had been too long since my body was pushed to move with any real level of speed. Call me tortoise! Nevertheless, I couldn't stop until I made sure she was okay. My mind quickly created an image of me standing over an empty grave that I could only assume was hers. I would be alone. If she was gone, no one would be left for me.

"NANA!" I burst through the door, yelling her name so loudly that it felt like the force of the sound would shred the inside of my throat.

Each room was hastily scanned as I dashed through the small house looking for her; but she was not there. Panicked, I stared out the window facing her backyard; hoped she would be there, sitting on her porch swing sipping tea like she often did. The empty swing only reinforced the image of the grave and made

18

it more resilient in my mind. I was alone. I fell to my knees ignoring the pain that shot through them as they smashed against the floor.

What did it matter now if I fell apart? She was no longer here. I was alone. For a moment I questioned my sanity, why did this cause me so much angst? So what, it was just one missed one call, one voicemail unheard. Did that mean she was gone? There was no logical explanation for the feeling, but inside I knew that I was losing her, if I hadn't already. The tears began to build up in my eyes, blurring my vision. I made no attempt to stop them from spilling freely over the rim as I fell deeper into the abyss; the loneliness eating me up and swallowing me whole. Why hadn't I taken the time to be with her? Why didn't I try to be closer to her? Was I so worried about my mother condemning my actions that I allowed it to make me neglect the only person left in this world who meant anything to me?

My self-criticizing thoughts were broken by a sound that sparked my hopes. Glasses knocked against each other, ringing from the cellar that I forgot existed. Again my tired body was forced to me; lifting to my feet and walking to the door in the kitchen that led to down into the old brick crypt. When I was younger my mother told me she kept old bones and witchy things down there, it took four years for Nana to get me down there without inducing tears, but it still gave me the creeps.

I froze; my hand gripping the doorknob with so much pressure that I felt my fingers would turn to dust.

What if she is hurt, or dead, or… I stopped my thoughts and searched to regain the hope that had overcome me with the chimes of the moving glass from beneath and when I heard the glasses knocking around again, I focused on the sound, opened the door with one last push, and ran down the stairs.

Three

The pounding of my heart slowed to a more even rhythm at the sight of her kneeling down on the cellar floor digging through some old crates. It was hard to believe she was nearly 70 years old. I was envious of her. My grandmother was determined to stay as fit as possible. She was thin with the body of a runner. Even in her old age she was more active than I was, taking part in charity runs, triathlons and working with Habitat for Humanity building homes for the less fortunate. She was a woman to be awed.

My body was crashing, going into shock as my heart rate slowed. The natural energy boost that came from the adrenaline rush produced by my fear had begun to fade. She was safe; there was no need for panic. Now my body sounded its' alarm. I had pushed myself too far. I stumbled, and reached for the railing by the steps, that groaned under my weight.

"Oh," my grandmother turned toward me as my vision began to blur, the world around me became shaded at the edges. "Alexa, what are you doing here?"

She pulled herself up with wide eyes and rushed to my side. That was the last thing I remembered before everything went black. As the world closed in, I forced the pain that spread through my limbs, out of my mind.

When consciousness returned with the feeling of lightheadedness, the dark basement was longer my surroundings, instead my grandmother's bed cradled my stiff body. The only thing visible from my position was all the dust collectors that lined a tall shelving unit. There were dozens of them; little figurines and ceramic pieces covered every flat surface of the room, I remembered them well. My grandmother was a real pack rat, but she swore that every piece told a story, taught a lesson, and held a deeper meaning for her. As a child, I would pick up random pieces and ask her to tell me their story. It never failed. Every story was different and magically intriguing, even if I didn't completely believe them.

I hadn't been inside my grandmother's home for nearly three years. Even after my parents died, she always came to me; it was never the other way around. Taking in the scent of her, feeling the warmth of her bed and hearing the soft hum as she approached the bedroom door, I felt guilty. Too stiff to move, the only option was to wait for her to come. Movement wasn't going to be a welcomed activity anyway. As it was, the pull and push of the air that entered my lungs was painful enough. That regret I mentioned earlier, yeah, it was kicking in.

REVITALIZED

My grandmother entered the room carrying a small tray in her hands. The aroma of green tea and honey followed her and filled the room. I watched her carefully as she walked; every moment was graceful and effortless, even in the simplest of things. Even in sitting the tray down she looked refined, as if she had practiced the movement for years: the study of place setting. Sometimes it looked like she was floating rather than walking. The ground was not deserving of touching her feet.

"Finally, her eyes are open," she said smiling at me. My attempt to return the expression failed. It didn't seem possible for the muscles in my face to hurt so much.

"You're okay," my voice croak as she approached the bed. "I thought something was wrong." My mind flooded with images of my rush to make it to her, to save her from nothing at all, my agony as I searched for her, with thoughts of standing over her grave, and then falling and apparently passing out.

"Well, why on earth would you think that?" She smiled around the ageless voice and pretended she couldn't hear the panic in my mine.

"You didn't call!" I shouted, or did what was as close to a shout as my body would allow. I frowned, and for a moment questioned my own attitude. Once again, the concern was there, why had the lack of a phone call had gotten to me so much? I was furious with her and I couldn't comprehend why. She was okay, not hurt or worse. I should have been happy or at least relieved, but I wasn't. Why?

I'd never felt that way towards her before, or anyone at all. There was a fire inside me, this overwhelming intensity that filled my mind. My heart started to race with the return of that all too familiar, yet strange pulling in the pit of my stomach, the one I'd run away from. The fear that usually accompanied the tugging sensation came back with a resilient force and smacked at the side of my head, shaking me to my core. I looked at her, and waited for her to answer me.

With an intentional lack of speed, she finished her approach to the bed. I doubt I had ever seen her move so leisurely before. She always moved with purpose even if was in that airy way, it was never a wasted effort. The decision to take her time did not help my rage. If anything, it only infuriated me more.

"Now, calm down, Alexa," she looked at me cool as ever. Her eyes were as calm as her voice. In her hand she held a damp towel which she used to dab my forehead. It wasn't until the cool moisture touched me that I realized how hot I was. She leaned back to look me in the eye. "Better?"

I rolled my eyes, staring at the shelf behind her. She was doing it again. She knew what was happening with me. This weird thing, pulling at my insides that was trying to rip me apart, yet she acted like she had no idea. She always did. She kept on pretending even when I stopped asking her for an explanation.

"I didn't call, because I assumed you no longer wanted me to." Her words were steady, but I didn't believe her. There was something more that she was not telling me.

It was a lie and we both knew it! She had never compromised for anyone before. Even after my mother was gone, she still pressed me about 'black magic', although she hated when I called it that. She always held onto the hope that it was my mother who rejected her ways with such conviction, and that my heart would eventually become open to the possibilities.

"The real reason?" I asked, staring her directly in the eye. As soon as I did, I immediately regretted it. Her deep chocolate brown eyes always snatched me into them. I felt as though all thoughts escaped my mind and I was calm. For a split second, I had almost forgotten about the inexplicable rage building inside me. I struggled to pull my gaze from hers.

She blinked long and hard, deliberately releasing me from their pull. I was free. I fixed my eyes on the quilt she had placed over my legs. It was my favorite and she knew it. I always envied her nimble fingers and the way she crocheted the most amazing designs and patterns I had ever seen. As athletic as I was, my fingers were clumsy, and I more than often dropped things. I never tried to learn how to crochet. I always figured it would be a pointless attempt.

"Well," she sighed "I am leaving." She stared off into space. Her face was now blank and void of all emotion as if she hadn't said anything at all.

"What do you mean…leaving?" I nearly choked on the word. My anger was momentarily silenced, and the fear of a lonely abyss slowly began to wrap itself around me again.

She sat on the edge of the bed, and handed me a cup of warm tea. "This will help you to relax." She said nodding her head at my rigid fingers that were clawing at the quilt. "I have to go dear. I wish I could explain further, but I cannot. My time here with you is over. I only wish I had been able to…" she trailed off; locked in her own mind. The features of her face were frozen in the moment.

I wanted her to finish explaining what could possibly be so important that she had to leave me. The words wouldn't come, all I could do was stare at her, and try to etch the image of her face on the surface of mind. There weren't many pictures of her, how would I remember? Her hair was long and black. The straight length almost touched the bed even as she sat straight up. There was only the slightest hint of gray sprinkled throughout it. Her honey tinted skin the same as my mother's, the same as my own. It was then that I noticed how much she looked like my mother; how much they shared. They could have been twins. I started to imagine that this is what my mother would have come to look like if she had lived, but those thoughts were to painful to continue. To have to think of losing my mom and grandmother both, I could not handle that. I took a deep breath, inhaling her and noting the levels of her scent. The tinges of wildflower, mint, and incense were cataloged along with my mother's pancakes. I refused to let her go.

"Able to what?" anxious, I had to know what was happening in her mind.

"Nothing…it's too late now, anyway. Just relax dear. Everything will be fine," her words were confusingly mechanical, almost robotic, and sounded as though she was reading from a script. This was not my grandmother speaking, but why would she lie? What could she be hiding? She smiled a weary smile, one I had never seen the muscles of her face curve to create. I was hit again with the heat of fury.

"You know, I am getting really tired of your riddles," I growled through my teeth. What was this evil coming from within me? My thoughts were ones of concern, was she hurt, ill? How could I help? Instead, the ridiculous response slipped from between my lips and despite the obvious challenges, I was up on my feet. Anger blocked out the pain in my body, as I stormed out the door. She mumbled something under her breath as I walked away, it was too low to really make any sense of it. Knowing her it was likely some warning about my health and wellbeing, either way, I didn't care.

I slammed the front door behind me so hard it shook the thin walls surrounding it. The whimsical garden was lost on me, my only concern was getting away from her. The engine of my old car sputtered to life and without checking to see if she'd followed me, I threw it in gear drove away. I had no idea where I was going; home was not an option. That would be the first place she would go if she decided it was worth the effort to come after me. No, I had to get away from her. It was what she wanted, to be away from me, to leave me alone.

Four

I drove around for hours going nowhere in particular; my only thought was to outrun the pain; not the physical, but the emotional. It was difficult, feeling like I was so far outside of myself, and barely able to distinguish my own face as I glanced in the rearview mirror. There was something strange about my eyes, the color seemed different. My effort to pinpoint the change failed because I couldn't seem to remember what my true eye color was. I shut them tight and shook my head; hurling away the thought. How could I forget my own eye color? It was a ridiculous thought that only worried me more. The internal debate began, would be beneficial to turn the car around, go back, and face her? Would that stop me from losing my mind? Part of me wanted to see her, that part begged me to turn around and do everything in my power to stop her from leaving. What if I never saw her again? The other part, still boiling with unexplained anger, knew on a deeper level that if I went back, I wouldn't like what I would find.

This new side of myself was completely unrecognizable; it was reckless and scary. I drove without looking at the road, much faster than the posted speed limit. I often shut my eyes just trying to untangle the web inside my mind. My fingers tightened around the steering wheel, to stop my hands from shaking, and to focus on something other than my rampant thoughts. The car stopped in a location that was familiar, one that hadn't been visited in a long time, but the recollection was instant. Parked at the edge of Lake Michigan, I questioned how I got there. Hell, it hadn't even registered to me that the car was moving down Lake Shore Drive. How did I manage to navigate the dangerously curvy road without crashing? Even when I didn't have my eyes shut, the road ahead had not been my focal point.

The small park that was just barely within my range of view across the lot brought a smile to my face. This was the backdrop to many Saturday afternoons as a child with my mother and father. It was exactly how I recalled it, frozen in time, yet everything surrounding it looked different. The buildings that touched the sky were all new and improved. However, it was still the same quiet place I loved coming to. It had the same metal swing set and jungle gym, only with a fresh coat of red and blue paint. The sprinklers where I ran in my bathing suit, because I was too afraid to go into the lake, the sandbox where I spent countless hours perfecting my sand castles, the path where I rode my bike and scraped my knee countless times, they were all the same.

I pictured him, my father, strong yet loving hands pushed me on the swing. A high pitched laughter rang out from my mouth as my mother stood in front of us making crazy faces and funny noises. Behind my mother was the picnic she'd carefully laid out on the grass as my father and I ran around playing tag. I could hear his voice echoing in my mind. He said nothing in particular, but it was his voice. The tenor of it wrapped around me tightly; a blanket of security.

The anxiety melted away with the images of my family and left me calm. I rolled the windows down to allow the cool air coming off the lake to brush against my face, as I gazed out at the little playground. It chilled my skin and reached deeper than the surface; calming the fires that raged within me. Finally at ease, I remained in my car. My eyes focused on the waves in the water, making me feel as if I would float away momentarily. My chest rose and fell with the tide and the car filled with the scent of the water. As I further relax into myself, I thought about my mom. Her smile, her laugh, her eyes were floating in the air in front of mine. Tears fell from my eyes but they were not inspired by sorrow.

Were the tears for my mother, my father, or for me? Assuming the wind was the cause for the salty streaks that fell down my face, I closed my eyes, but they continued; pushed forward by a source deep within me. The emotion there was something I didn't understand, but I accepted it. I let it consume me because it felt better than trying to deny it. I stopped trying to figure out what was causing my tears, and rolled my windows up to a crack just to keep the air in the car cool. Ignoring the empty feeling that seemed to only instigate my tears, I closed my eyes, and let the sound of the waves carry me away.

I was at peace, my mind away from the world, and all the problems waiting for me. This moment of mental harmony was annoyingly interrupted by a tapping; an irritating, relentless, tapping against the window. I tried to ignore it but I was unable to block the aggravation from my mind. I reluctantly opened my eyes, but was forced to quickly shut them. There was a bright light pointed directly at my face. I groaned and held my hand up to shield myself from the visual assault.

"Are you okay, Miss?" The park ranger asked, tapping his finger against my window again. His voice was low and shaky; indicating that he was someone much older.

"Yeah," I struggled to say. My throat was bone dry and the word croaked from within me. I put my hand in front of my eyes, to block out the blinding light.

REVITALIZED

"It's after midnight, Miss, the park is closed. I'm going to have to ask you to move along," he pulled down the light affording me my first glimpse of his face. He was an older man of at least 60 with scraggly, gray hair in his eyebrows. He wore a security uniform, blue and baggy over his frail frame. I wondered why he was still working at his age, which lead me back to thoughts of my grandmother and her vow to stay active right up until the day she died. An empowering yet disheartening thought.

I winced as I recalled the trip that got me to my lakeside getaway, and the force that drove me to this place; my safety zone. It was the shock on her face as I threw that ridiculous temper tantrum and stormed out of her home that was highlighted in my memory.

I had to get to her. I had to apologize. If she was going to leave I wouldn't have our last moment together be one with me acting so irrationally. I turned the key in the ignition and started the car. The older man was staring at me with worry in his eyes. I smiled and waved as I drove away; not wanting to even think about why he was looking at me like that. I knew I must have looked bad, and was surprised he didn't try to drug test me. There were so many assumptions to be made, drunken drug addict, runaway, etc. I hoped he wasn't calling the police.

As I drove away my intention was to go to her house to face her and get this embarrassing ordeal over with. It would mean crawling back to her and pleading for forgiveness. I looked at the clock in my dashboard. It was nearly one in the morning. I had slept in my car for an entire day! My sad show of remorse would have to wait until tomorrow; I tried not to be too happy with this realization. Hey, I wasn't just being a coward, she was old, active or not, it meant she would be sleeping, and it would be rude to show up at such a late hour. It was simply a bonus that gave me an excuse to put off what was sure to be a horribly awkward conversation.

How was I supposed to explain my actions? Even worse, how could I justify my rage? I couldn't even make sense of it in my own head. As hard as I tried to make it all fit, it just didn't. Nothing about what happened was right. It was like I was a different person. I had never blown up on anyone like that; especially not her. Even with her quirky superstitions and weird artifacts lying all over her house, my grandmother was the most loving and most accepting woman I knew. Thinking of her face now, all I felt was happiness and relief because she was okay which is what should have mattered to me before. She was healthy and alive and that's what I wanted.

The drive home was a ride on the mental, self-abusive, rollercoaster. So, what if she moved, she was alive and I could always visit her wherever she decided to go. I wondered where that would be, knowing her, it was probably somewhere off the radar. I seriously would have to start taking better care of myself though. No way could I take a trip anywhere with my body so broken down. The physicality of just this one day had my bones feeling as if they were ready to snap.

I had to laugh at myself. In the haste of my overreaction was the neglect to take into full consideration the generally sedentary state of my life. There I was acting like a new age version of superwoman, flying off to save the day. Every nerve in my body shouted at me, punctuating the thought. Idiot! The muscles in my arms tensed and my fingers ached from being wrapped around the steering wheel so tightly. I had to alternate hands for the remainder of the drive. I was 30 minutes away from home, and an hour away from a relaxing warm bath, which I needed more than ever.

The summer air warmed my body as I moved further from the chill of the lake. The extended exposure to the cool lake air was not the greatest idea I'd ever had, but it's not like I planned on sitting in my car for nearly 12 hours! Lucky for me, it was a warm summer night in Chicago and the heat provided a bit of relief. I drove back to the quiet suburban area where my home was. No matter how many times I witnessed it, I never got over how weird it was, going from the lively streets of the city to the dreary blocks of the suburbs. Each time I made the transition between the two, I got the feeling of someone flicking a light switch off. Even at nearly 2AM, the city was still alive. Music played in the distance, and the smell of an all-night BBQ joint jolted my senses and reminded me of the emptiness of my stomach.

Driving into my neighborhood, the streets were dead. No noise, no underlying rhythm, just the sound of a train passing somewhere off in the distance. The only light was provided by the dimly lit streetlights and random windows of the homes that belonged to night owls.

The final approach to my house provided a painful embarrassment. It was hard to look at, my home, the eyesore of the neighborhood. The grass was long and thick with weeds that grew even longer and were starting to sprout up over the sidewalk. The paint on the siding was faded and cracked. The shutters on the windows, knocked around by the winter winds, were barely hanging on. I looked away ashamed; my father would have been disgusted to see our home in this condition. He would be so disappointed in me.

Having a garage that was attached to the house made it easier to ignore these obvious structural flaws. My dad decided to build the addition right after we moved into the house; he felt it was safer for my mother and me. The walk from the curb to the front door would surely be too dangerous without him there. Especially in the rough streets of Naperville! He was overly protective in that way. If we could have pulled up right into the living room, direct from car to couch, he would have made it happen.

Viewing my home in that light, dim and barely visible, it looked more like a haunted house pulled straight out of a horror film, than the warm home it was meant to be. It was hard to imagine what this old colonial house used to look like when I was younger. It was beautiful in its simplicity (not including the intricate carvings of course) and it stood out on the street for completely different reasons than it did now. What was once appreciation could now be disgust or possibly even sympathy for the lost girl living within its broken walls.

I pulled into the garage, stepped out of the car and crept into the house. My body felt heavy, as if my limbs were made of solid iron. On my way through the house and up to my bathroom, I gradually became more aware of all the things I had blocked out.

Trash was piled up, overflowing from nearly every receptacle. It seemed the only one I had bothered to empty was the one in the kitchen, for obvious reasons. All the plants were crunchy, brown, and dead. Dust covered every surface. Even the pictures on the wall that I stopped and stared at every day looked strangely broken. The smiles they held looked dull and lifeless. Their frames were crooked and faded.

I couldn't believe this was my home, my mother's sanctuary, and my father's work of art. It was falling apart around me. My mind was so wrapped up in grieving and feeling sorry for myself, that all of it had gone unnoticed. I found the picture that had greeted me that morning; it too was covered in a film of gray that I'd somehow been able to block from my mind. Eyes half open, as I tried not to notice any more flaws that surrounded me, I progressed to my room. Each point of distress reached out and latched onto my body, dragging my spirit down making it even harder to walk; harder to breathe.

The bathroom was across the hall from my room, the only other room I took good care of besides the kitchen. Possibly because I always had a major issue with public washrooms and I couldn't have my own looking or smelling like one. I turned on the water, and sat on the edge of the tub making sure it began to fill, sometimes the stopper slipped. There's nothing more disappointing than returning to what you think will be a nice full warm bath and finding a cold empty tub.

Once satisfied that my bath would fill, I moved to the medicine cabinet, took out my bottle of Tylenol 3, and popped two in my mouth, against the doctors' note that said one every eight hours as needed, and swallowed them dry. I grabbed the glass sitting on the edge of the sink, filled it halfway with cool water, and poured it down my throat. I peeled off my clothing slowly, hoping to avoid any muscle spasms, and tossed them in the laundry basket. There was another issue, laundry. I thought about the dirty clothes piling up in the corner of my room. I was so out of touch with reality that I hadn't even bothered to put them in the hamper.

I loved this room; my mother let me redecorate it after I turned 16. It was my own sanctuary. The walls were blue, with clouds painted on the ceiling. It reminded me of when I was younger, I would sit on the hood of my dad's car and watch the sky. I spent hours in my own world, making out shapes that passed by in the clouds. The strange thing was that every time I looked at this ceiling I felt like I was viewing a new sky, new clouds, and new shapes. I never figured out how my mom got it to do that, but I thanked her so much for it. I climbed into the ready tub and sighed deeply at the instant relief that passed over me once my body became submerged. I wiggled my toes and fingers in the water trying to ease the tension out of my muscles.

I felt calm and was relaxed again; just as I was at the lake. The silence that filled the house was eerie, and yet somehow it helped put me more at ease. The loneliness was comforting in its familiarity. My head was finally clear again. I focused on the clouds above my head hoping to keep the negative thoughts from flooding back and it worked. I was able to push them from my mind and lock them outside.

"Thanks mom," I sighed as I began to drift off to the sweet unconscious world I loved.

I closed my eyes and let my mind coast and fell into the fantasy of my grandmother's miracle cure, one I often enjoyed; I mean who wouldn't at least toy with the idea of instant recovery? I was running, going nowhere, just running. It felt amazing. Every part of my body was working in unison, working as a team instead of clamoring against each other. The breeze rushed across my face and I smiled wide, grinning from ear to ear. Off in the distance were my friends, all the people left behind when I decided to drop out of life. They were laughing and waiting for me, calling me to come over. I waved at them and started to run faster.

I was closing in on them when the ground beneath my feet turned into a thick mud. I tried to run harder and faster, but the more effort put into escaping, the deeper my legs became lodged into the mud. Barely moving now, sinking, I screamed for help, but no one came. I descended deeper still and could see them, turning their backs on me, forgetting my presence completely.

I opened my mouth to scream again, but the black mud spilled between my jaw, filling my lungs and drowning me. My body was no longer moving. My arms refused to aid in my efforts to climb out of the pit. The darkness was growing around me. I looked up just in time to see the last bit of light closing off as I was dragged deeper into the hole.

My eyes shot open to the blue skies above me as I gasped for air, and reached out around me to find something solid to hold onto. I couldn't drown alone in my tub, who would find me? When my hand touched the smooth side of the tub, I realized there was nothing to fear. I took a deep breath and released it slowly, attempting to move myself back to the calm I had achieved before.

The water in the tub was still warm. The jets built into the sides had done their job. Despite the nerve-wracking dream, I felt relaxed and my body was at ease again. I splashed some water on my face and wiped it away with a facecloth. It had been so long since I had dreamt or had any evidence of an active subconscious. It was a side effect of the medication, which the doctor told me would happen. Nearly a year without a dream, and now I was having a nightmare.

Five

Once the water began to cool, I carefully climbed out of the tub, grabbed a towel, wrapped it around myself, and headed for my room. I made a mad dash across the hall to avoid another dose of crappy homemaker shame. My stomach growled at me while I dressed. My outfit of choice was an oversized t-shirt and old gym shorts. I hadn't eaten since my bowl of fruit this morning, which had been thrown half eaten in the sink. I settled for the box of crackers in my nightstand. They were always there for the nights my stomach refused to calm, which happened more times than not because of the pills that waited for me in the kitchen.

I chomped on a few crackers while searching for the TV remote. After I found it on the floor under the nightstand, (note to self, stop tossing the remote after turning the TV off at night), I propped myself up on the bed, and began my usual channel hop. Nothing was on, of course, a thousand channels and there was never anything to watch. I landed on Nick at Night. They were running an all-night marathon of The Nanny. It was one of my favorites, most likely because Fran Fine reminded me so much of my best friend Jazz, fashion forward and full of spunk. I started to think of her, what had caused her abrupt need to have me back in her life? I watched a few episodes, never completely focusing on any of them, and then put the TV on mute.

I had almost forgotten that she had called earlier. The ordeal with my grandmother took over my mind for the day. It was clear that she wanted to reconnect, even though I figured that by now she would have replaced me as her best friend. Admittedly it was comforting to know that people were still thinking of me and that I hadn't been completely erased from their minds. Maybe I could reach back out to her. Nana would be leaving soon, and it was nice to think that I would have someone there.

The light from the images that flashed across the screen of my 42-inch television danced across the walls of my bedroom like a rhythmic ballet of colors. I sighed and started staring at the ceiling again. My eyes followed each cracked line until it faded out and then started on a new one. I was sure sleep would evade me; I would be tracing those cracks until the sun came up. After sleeping in the car for the day, there was no sense in hoping to get to sleep, or so I thought. Minutes later I was out cold and thankfully there were no more dreams.

The next morning, I woke up in the same way as before. I got out of bed still attempting to ignore my environment, but created a mental checklist of things to tackle for the day. First, I would go to my grandmother and apologize for my idiotic behavior, and then I would come home and call around to find someone, a professional, who could help me clean up the mess I had made of my home before returning the call from Jazz. I got dressed and headed down the stairs.

On my way to the kitchen, the mental list expanded. Paint of course, lots of dusting, sweeping, vacuuming, and all the dead plants had to be tossed. It was a wonder I could even breathe in this house with the stench of death and decay surrounding me. Perhaps I would stop on the way home to pick up some living plants.

I grudgingly took my pills again. There were no messages waiting on my answering machine. Nana must have been really upset with me; it was to be expected. I only hoped I could come up with an apology good enough to make her forgive me. It was hopeless; hell, I didn't even have an explanation for myself. I grabbed an apple and a bottle of water and headed for my car.

The trip took a half hour. I drove the exact speed limit, while crunching into the apple and going over my apology in my head. What could I say? Sorry I acted like a child and ran out yesterday? It was the only thing that resembled an appropriate apology, and yet it was still nowhere near what I felt I needed to say. All I could say was that I didn't know what had come over me and that was the truth.

The shorter the distance to her house got, the more nervous I became which caused the butterflies to swarm violently in my stomach. I tried to focus on her usually compassionate eyes. She would forgive me, she had to. I thought of her smile and had no doubt that she would understand, even if she wouldn't admit it. That was the thing about her; she had a way of knowing and understanding more about you than you ever did.

I rounded the corner and parked in front of her house. I had to double check the address because the house looked completely different, it looked normal. The overload of decorations was missing from the front yard. The plastic birds, garden gnomes, and wind chimes were all gone. Had she already started to pack? Even the flowers looked different. They drooped in a pathetic way, as if they had no access to the sun, even though it shone brightly overhead. Maybe, I was just projecting, giving the flowers feelings that were my own. I wanted anyone or anything to feel my anxiety and sadness, because no matter what, I would still be losing her. Misery loves company, even if that company is a pathetic looking plant.

I walked up to the door. Taking a deep breath, I reached for my key; going over the words again in my head but the door was unlocked and slightly cracked. I pushed the door aside and stepped into the house. As I crossed over the threshold my heart stopped; frozen mid-pump.

Everything was gone.

I walked through the abandoned rooms. They were all empty. If I hadn't just seen her, I wouldn't have believed she had ever been there at all. No furniture, no senseless artifacts. The walls that had previously been covered in pictures were all bare. The floors were too, even the carpet was gone. The dream catchers that usually hung in every doorway were all missing. My heart skipped another beat; pausing just long enough to make me fear it would never start again.

How could she have been gone? Overnight she had cleared out and vanished. The place even smelled different, the air was stale and dry, it was as if someone had been hired to come through and wash away every indication that she had ever existed. I sat on the floor with my back against the wall, I pulled my knees tight into my chest, and propped my head on my knees covering my eyes.

The tears flowed relentlessly. As I sat there I pressed my palms against my eyes, hard enough to leave bruises. Maybe, if I sat here long enough everything would return to the way I remembered it; the way it was just 24 hours ago. I would open my eyes, she would be here, and everything would return with her. She would float in with a tray of iced tea and smile at me. I would be able to apologize for treating her so poorly and everything would go back to normal. I would get a chance to make it all up to her. We would arrange her departure; I would be helpful and supportive. I would make this easier for both of us.

My cell phone vibrated in my pocket, but I ignored it. I could not break my concentration, not that I thought it would work, but for a moment I gave in to the hope of magic. I sat there longer, eyes still held tight, focusing on her face. As impossible as it sounded, it had to work. I opened my eyes; of course, nothing had changed at all. I had to leave. It wasn't the same place anymore. It was no longer the warm home that welcomed me and invited me to explore the mysteries inside. It was a shell, hollow and empty, and it was beginning to close in on me. I had to get out before it trapped me inside forever. She was gone.

On the drive back to my house, all the optimism I woke up with had been effectively drained away. I pulled into my garage, turned the car off, and just sat there. The tears had left their salty trails down my face. I stared at my dried-out reflection in the rear-view mirror. I was alone. There was no life left in my eyes; no warmth in my face. The little bit that I managed to hold on to over the last couple of years had left with her.

Once inside the house I headed straight for the kitchen. The one place I felt would help me, where my mother's embrace, her love, still waited for me. After fumbling with the keys to open the door, pushing the heavy wood aside, I froze in the doorway unable to carry myself any further. My breathing stopped, my muscles seized. I could feel my eyes widening;

stretching to the point of pain. My mouth fell open releasing a huff of air and it felt as if my heart was attempting to escape through the opening. She was here? For moment I became excited until I processed what I saw in front of me.

The table in the center of the room, the one I avoided like the plague, had been wiped clean of its dust covering, on its surface sat a green box with a white card marked, 'Alexa'. It sat in the center of the table; my dad's intricate designs sprawling out around it. It was her handwriting on the card. She had that kind of unmistakable penmanship, even from across the room I recognized it, slightly shaky, but still beautiful and clear; much better than my own.

Why? This was the only question my frazzled mind could formulate. Why had she placed this thing, whatever it was, in the one place she knew I couldn't touch? Was this some kind of test? How could she do this to me? As I looked at the table, it started to pull further and further away. I had to know what was inside that box. However, I felt as if my feet were glued to the floor. My legs wouldn't move, and my arms couldn't stretch far enough. It felt as though the table was moving away from me. Leaving me like everything else. Was this my curse? Everyone and everything I loved, needed, or wanted would be repelled from me.

Six

$\mathfrak{T}$ime lost its meaning as I measured the obstacle placed in my way. I remember distinctly telling her multiple times how hard it was for me to even look at that table let alone touch it. I could only imagine that this was her attempt at teaching me a lesson. I refused to believe my grandmother had done this intentionally just to pay me back for the pain that I had caused her the day before. She couldn't be so spiteful! That same inexplicable rage began to fill my insides. This time it was intensified by the idea of her betrayal, it grew faster than before. I needed to focus on staying calm, but it seemed stronger than before.

I walked over to the table and screamed at the box in the center of it. A powerful shriek that ripped from me so loudly that it shook my entire body, strangled my torso, and left no air in my lungs. The room was starting to spin. "Pull it together, Alexa!" I yelled at myself as I raged an internal battle of will, my own will against this unknown entity inside of me.

It seemed the more I tried to calm myself, the more the fury grew inside of me; completely counterproductive. It flared out like the tentacles of a wild flower, if I believed in magic; I would use those flames to destroy the box. Entertaining that thought only made my problem worse, adding more fuel to the fire.

My breath grew heavier with each passing moment, each pull of air felt weighed down as if it were mixed with dirt and sand. My skin burned and every muscle in my body tightened, threatening to lock up. I screamed again, this time the sound was louder and more strained. What the hell was happening to me? How could I let a table mess with my head so much? It was an inanimate object after all, I had to break whatever this hold, or more like repulsion, was that it had on me.

Somewhere buried inside of me had to be enough strength and courage to grab the box and read the card. I refused to be so weak that I would let an irrational fear stand between me and a message from my grandmother. She could have needed my help and had left me some sort of clue of where to find her. The unlikely thought of her needing my help was all it took to crush the fear. Remember me, the broken-down Wonder Woman.

I moved towards the table, blocking out images of shared meals and memories of my parents. With one swift move I snatched the box off the table quickly. I managed to barely touch the table; just the tip of my finger grazed the carving in the surface as I grabbed the box. Even that tiny second of contact shot a stinging pain straight up my arm. I ignored the feeling and opened the box first. Inside, was an odd little glass vial filled with a blue liquid, thick and shimmering, like molten crystal.

The bottle was shaped like two hearts; molded like an hourglass and twisted together in the middle. The stopper looked like a flame frozen in time. The metallic paint made it look almost real. There were three symbols etched in the glass; top, middle and bottom. I flipped the bottle over and over in my hand and tried to recognize the symbols, they felt familiar, but I had no idea what they were.

They looked like something ancient, but they just reminded me of Nana. She had little things like this all over her house, but this one; I had never seen before. It reminded me of how I found her yesterday; this could have been the glass she was looking for. I gave up trying to pull the symbols from the recesses of my mind and quickly grabbed the card off the table, this time avoiding all contact with the wooden surface.

Inside the card, written in the same shaky script of my grandmother's, was a note:

My dearest Alexa,
How I wish I could stay with you, but I am afraid my time here is up. I wish I could explain, but I cannot. Please take this gift from me. I know that you may not want it, but it is all I have to offer you. If you ever decide to accept your destiny and get past this aversion to my way of life, drink it and it will heal your body and give you the life you deserve. The life you were always meant to have.
Love always,
Nana

I thought the note, her words, would calm it; but no, they did the exact opposite. I felt myself losing control again. Her last words to me, and she uses them to press the issue of magic on me. She was leaving me alone with nothing and still had the nerve to continue with her agenda. I felt betrayed; stabbed in the back by my own grandmother. Didn't she care?! Didn't she know that without her I would be totally alone? There was no one else in my life. Just her, and she was tossing me aside as if I didn't matter at all. To think that I was going to apologize to her, to try and find a way to make it work where we could both be happy; it made me sick to my stomach.

I slammed the box back on the table, not thinking of my old fear of it. Once the box was out of my hand, the rage simmered, and the tears poured out with accompanying sobs. It was official. I was completely alone. What was the point of it all? There was no reason to be afraid of the table, or anything else in my life. Even if it came to life and tore me to shreds for having the nerve to lay a hand on it; at this point, I felt like it would be for the best. It would be a sweet release from my broken world.

I spent the next few days in my bed. I neglected to take my medication and barely made the effort to roll from side to side. What was the point? I kept asking myself this question every time I came anywhere near getting out of bed. I could just waste away to nothing. It wasn't as if I had anyone or anything here for me. There was no need for me to stay alive. No one would miss me. No one would truly care. I didn't need to be told it was self-pity. I knew it and accepted it.

The windows were completely blocked out by the thick black drapes that my mother had installed for the times that I needed to sleep during the day. I wanted to be disconnected from the world. Not to mention the sun piercing through the windows was blindingly bright and made my head spin. The darkness that my mother's gift provided made it easier to lay in my bed counting my woes while surrounded by nothingness.

My cell phone rang, well vibrated, after what felt like the hundredth call I switched it to vibrate. Yes, I know I could have turned the ringer off entirely, but it appeared that some part of me was holding on to the need for my existence to matter. Each time the phone vibrated, it told me that someone knew and cared that I was there. No, just because I wanted people to care doesn't mean I wanted to actually talk to them. That would interfere with my self-loathing. I thought by now the battery would have died. Whoever was calling was being persistent. I grunted and threw in the towel; it was obvious they were not going to give up. I picked up the phone and flipped it open. Yes my phone, much like everything else in my life, was outdated. It was Jazz.

Maybe I could talk to her one last time. This would give me the chance to leave her with a better impression of me before my lifeless corpse was found decaying in my bed.

"Hello?" My voice sounded dry. I hadn't spoken a word since the screaming that left my throat bruised and my voice strained. The sound barely made it past my lips.

"Finally! I have been calling you for days," there was a mixture of panic and relief in her voice.

"What's up Jazz?" It felt good to hear her voice. It was refreshing. I tried to make my voice sound more alive, but I failed.

"Did you forget my b-day bash? You know I have it every year, and now that I got my new place, you have to be here! I gave you a pass last year, but that's not going to happen this time around," all sound of panic was gone. All it ever took was the mentioning of a party and Jazz would be unable to concentrate on anything else.

"Oh...I don't know Jazz; I'm not really feeling up to doing anything. It's been a rough few days," the thought of being jammed up against drunken strangers made my voice crack even more.

"Oh, no you don't, you listen girl; you have been missing in action for far too long now. I was being easy on you because," she stopped the words from coming out, "well, you know why, but I want my best friend back now."

"I don't know…." I started to whine, but she cut me off.

"Alexa, we miss you and we want you back. It's not just me, it's all of us. I know you are going through a lot right now, and I heard your grandmother up and left. My mom told me, you know she been keeping tabs on you. You need us and we need you. Just let me be here for you, Lex," her words were full of sincerity. It sounded like she was holding back tears, but knowing Jazz, there would be no evidence of that on her face.

"It's okay, Jazz," I tried to comfort her. "You don't have to worry about me. I'm fine. I've been dealing with this for a long time on my own, I can handle it." I was not as strong as her; hearing her concern for me had initiated the waterworks. I was sure my voice painted the picture of my tear stained face.

"Oh, spare me the speech, drop the front, Lex," I could hear the aggravation in her voice. "Say you're coming and I'll stop nagging you. If you don't, I promise I will show up at your house, banging and screaming at your door, and physically drag you to the party. So, we can do this the easy way, or we can do this the hard way, but either way, your little butt will be at my party."

There was nothing more I could say, I knew she meant it. She had done it before. Freshman year in high school, I didn't have a date to the spring fling; she refused to let me sit around the house all sad and alone. She dumped her date and we went together, against my will.

"Okay, okay," I said overwhelmed. "When and where?" I couldn't believe I was giving in so fast. Maybe, I wasn't as ready to drop out of life as I tried to make myself believe. Perhaps I had been waiting for her to call all along.

Seven

She told me the time and gave me her new address, and reiterated that she would make sure I showed up one way or another, which apparently meant the possibility of her friend, 'Jay' coming to pull me from my bed by force. She made extra sure that I understood that Jay was a stocky guy who would have no trouble tossing me over his shoulder, fireman style. She made me repeat back the information twice before she would let me get off the phone.

The party was the next night at her new condo, just can't beat that advanced notice. Her dad promised her that he would get it for her after she graduated high school, and successfully made it through her first year of college. It took an entire year of looking to find a place, not because of him, but because Jazz was so picky. Yes, it was her dad's way of keeping tabs on her obviously, but there was no way she was turning down her own condo, or settling for something less than perfect.

Recuperation was out of the question, there just was not enough time. My muscles ached, over used, abused, and without medication I would be suffering.

Each nerve stepped up to voice their outrage resulting in a succession of spasms. I promised my friend that I would be there and I would. I didn't, however, promise to stay for any extended length of time. I would go and show my face, linger for five or ten minutes, and then escape out the door whenever she was distracted.

I ended the call, tossed the outdated phone to the other side of the bed, and pulled the covers over my head. What had I gotten myself into? I didn't feel like being around people, especially knowing that they would all be exuding obvious pity for me. Everyone already knew my situation; there was no way to avoid that embarrassment.

I was almost surprised about Jazz's mom knowing that Nana left, but it wasn't all that shocking. Jazz was nosy but her mom, well she had the biggest nose of them all, I'm talking top quality snoop. No matter where you were or what you were doing, she could sniff you out. Maybe, she was the reason my mother always knew when I would sneak away to my grandmother's house. She was a hound and apparently, a snitch.

My intention was to go back to sleep, but instead, I was compiling a to-do list. I became nauseous debating what I would wear, how to style my hair and the crowd of faces that would be staring at me and sizing me up. Would I remember all of their names? What if they didn't remember me? My mind went on rambling, until I had reached a level of certain paranoia.

REVITALIZED

Stress and anxiety started to form into a thick lump in my throat. It had been so long since I had been anywhere that required me to put any additional thought into my attire. Not to mention my hair, I hadn't done anything to that monster in months besides my messy ponytail. I touched my head feeling through the tangles and cringed at the idea of combing through them, that alone would leave me in need of a serious painkiller.

The decision was to lie in bed for the rest of the day, but I tried and failed to ignore the questions and worries that rattled around in my head. My inability to block out the noise, of course started me down the road to formulate an acceptable excuse for my sudden inability to attend. Surely, I could come up with something that would convince Jazz that my appearance at her party would be a bad idea. Unfortunately, I sucked at lying and each sad justification I concocted sounded flimsier than the last. It was pointless anyway, even if I had been able to create a sound reason, Jazz had no intention of letting me off the hook.

The night went by slowly as I drifted in and out of a state very close to, but not quite sleep. Every time I opened my eyes, I groaned at the clock that sat on my nightstand. Big bold red numbers told me the time. It felt as if it was counting down to doomsday. I reached out and flipped the face of the clock away from me.

Hours later, moments before the sun illuminated the sky, I decided to get up. I would to take as much time as possible to get ready. Hell, I would need as much time as possible to manage to look even mildly presentable. First thing I wanted to tackle was wardrobe. It was a surprise to find out how many options I had; too many options, which only made me feel worse. My closet was stocked with clothes that hadn't been worn in years, and the excess of options only added to my dilemma. How was it possible that I had such a massive heap of clothing waiting to be washed and yet there were still a hundred clean options for me to choose from? I didn't need anything else to stress me out, so I chose an outfit that I always felt confident in. I could use every bit of help I could get, when it was my turn to step up and face the firing squad. The fact that the outfit was comfortable was a plus.

I laid the faded denim pants and maroon strapless shirt on the bed, took a deep breath and moved on to shoes. Another overwhelming factor, I looked at the rows of pumps on the floor. Remembering how, despite my Tomboy nature, I loved to wear heels. I justified this contradiction by saying it was a good workout for the thighs and core, and it helped me with balance! Yes, I omitted the fact that I liked the way my legs looked and how guys noticed them as I walked by. It was a reaction you just couldn't get while wearing a pair of sneakers.

Jazz was the only one of our friends who knew the extent of my secret obsession, hell she's the one who started it. Freshman year, black chunky heels, she called them 'stacks'. She dared me to do a sprint in them. It was love at first kick off! There was a different shoe for almost every outfit. It was the only 'girly' thing I did in excess. My parents hadn't minded supporting my habit if I kept my grades up. I frowned at my favorite pair, a dark red pump that would look great with the outfit lying on my bed.

My ankles screamed at me, protesting in advance, the thought of attempting to balance in them for even a second. Giving up on that idea, I grabbed a pair of black flats and tossed them on the floor in front of the bed; I pulled out a strapless bra from the drawer to wear under my shirt, and threw it on top of the selection.

I glanced at the clock; 7:33. I had nearly 12 hours to kill before it would be time to leave. Too anxious to return to my bed, I decided I would distract myself. My body ached, but I needed to find something to do to stop myself from worrying about things that were out of my control. I wanted to pop a few pills, little tablets of relief, to block out the recurring spasms, headache and overall soreness, but if I were to take any medication now, it would have me knocked out in minutes and would unquestionably result in me breaking my promise to Jazz.

Looking around my room, I gave in to the urge to clean. It just had to be done. The clothing that was thrown on the floor, was picked up and tossed it into the wicker hamper, and pulled it out into the hall before moving on to tackle the large desk that sat in the corner opposite my bed. It had been so long since I turned on my laptop there were surely cobwebs on the keys. The desk was littered with papers and unopened junk mail. It took me nearly an hour to sort through the mess. In the end, I had a large shopping bag filled with what I decided was trash, and a desk I could see.

After organizing the items on my dresser, entertainment center, and vanity mirror, the one that my mom insisted every girl should have. It was not really my taste. She was mortified when she found out that I had covered the ivory finish in a coat of black paint with the Brahma Bull (yes, I love The Rock) on the tabletop. This was an act of rebellion that I regretted after about three months. The paint was stripped away, and my mom was only too eager to have it refinished.

I grabbed the bag of trash and headed downstairs. It was nearly one o'clock now and I still had so much time to kill. Content with continuing my cleaning spree, I went to the pantry and pulled out every dusting and disinfecting supply I could find. It was about time I utilized all the knowledge I had gained from hours of watching the DIY Network.

I went through the house. Scrubbing and polishing everything in my path, it was unnerving how much there was to do; talk about a slob, I had been living in filth and I hadn't even noticed it. By the time I was done, I had three Hefty bags filled with trash, used paper towels, and dead plants. I wasn't anywhere near done with everything, but it made me feel better that I had accomplished anything at all.

I sat in the front room of the house, the one room I had managed to get completely clean, while I waited for the kettle of tea on the stove to sound off. The sunlight glared through the window, and I could see my mom and dad again. They were sitting on the couch, across from the loveseat. They were together, holding hands and smiling at me. I felt comforted by the idea that they were proud of me. I was getting back into life, or at least attempting to. I would be sure to replace the plants to restore some life to the room.

The teakettle screeched from within the kitchen, effectively shredding the image in my head. I did have a moment of happiness, and though my body ached, I finally reached a certain level of calm. I went into the kitchen and pulled the kettle from the heat. I grabbed a mug from the cabinet above the sink and filled it with the hot tea. I closed my eyes and let the heat from the liquid tickle my nose as I blew on it to cool it before taking a sip. It warmed my body, and helped to relax my mind a bit more, and I sighed leaning back against the counter.

Hanging on the wall across from me was an old miniature grandfather clock, announcing that my time was up. With that announcement came the blow of all the nerves and anxiety I had worked so hard to forget returning to me. They effectively knocked the air out of my lungs. It was time to get ready, now I was running late. I thought I was on track, but at some point, time had slipped away. I longed for a warm bath to help me relax more, but there was only time for a quick shower. The party started at eight and it was an hours' drive to Jazz' new condo in downtown Chicago and I planned to get there early. It would make it that much easier to slip out when the rest of the crowd started to pour in.

I drank the remaining hot tea from my cup, faster than I should have, farewell to my taste buds. I rinsed the cup, and put it away before putting the left over the tea in the refrigerator. I checked to make sure that everything was put away and turned to leave the room. From the corner of my eye I could still see the box sitting on the table, and for a moment I thought of taking it. Maybe it could help me make it through this night without completely embarrassing myself. I shrugged the idea off with the thought of what my mother would say if she knew what I was considering. Whatever it was would be punctuated by a look of complete disgust. Still I grabbed it, quickly of course to avoid contact. I would stash it in my nightstand, at least this way I wouldn't have to see it every time I entered the kitchen. I wouldn't take it; I repeated this to myself as I carried the box. I wouldn't give in.

Looking in the mirror after my shower, I wished I had chosen something else to wear. The clothes that used to hug my body now hung from my frame. I hadn't realized how much weight I'd lost, yet another thing gone unnoticed. I pulled my hair up into a loose bun, allowing a few strands fall around my face. I hadn't made much effort in that department. I tried briefly to pull a comb through it and when the first tooth snapped, I gave up on that idea. Well, it was better than my usual messy ponytail. So much for putting my best foot forward; I would just have to settle for mildly presentable. The point was to get this over with, not to win the award for best dressed, and besides, if there was one; Jazz would beat me to it anyway. That would be like competing in a race with one leg against Sanya Richards, God how I loved her. She was my idol, my inspiration for running until...well that no longer mattered.

I tried my best to cover the flaws in my complexion with the foundation I'd found in the medicine cabinet. It was no use, my skin looked horrible, and the makeup was too old to do it any justice. It was a dry and blotchy, what frustration, the more I put on, the more I seemed to need. Considering the fact that the makeup was expired and not safe for any skin, especially skin that hadn't been taken care of, I decided to go au-naturel. Yes, scary I know! When my cell phone rang, I was washing the makeup from my face; I went into my room to pick it up from the charger where I'd left it. No sense in checking the caller I.D., I already knew who it was.

"Hey," I sighed momentarily revisiting the list of lacking excuses, this was my chance to avoid a terrible disaster, but I couldn't get a single apologetic syllable to cross my lips. I didn't want to disappoint Jazz, not on her birthday. Hell, not any day.

"I'm just checking to make sure you're not trying to back out on me." She sounded happy, genuinely excited to be able to see me again, and that helped ease my nerves, a little. At least there would be one person that was smiling at me out of love and not pity.

"I just finished getting dressed and I will be leaving in a few minutes." I smiled to myself. Despite the growing amount of nerves, I was looking forward to seeing her again. She was my best friend, my sister, my other half. We had always shared a bond that exceeded the levels of friendship and I missed that connection. That closeness to another human being, it was so important, too important to walk away from, again.

"Good! I will see you soon; I have to finish getting ready over here. Can't wait to see you, Lex," she sounded distracted by something clamoring in the background. Whatever it was, it must have been significant because she started yelling in Spanish. A language she only used when she was either very happy or very irritated, and by all the frustrated grunts, I could tell she hadn't suddenly become overwhelmed with glee.

"Thanks Jazz, you too," I hung up the phone laughing to myself at the mental image of the tirade she was on and the terrified looks of the workers. Jazz was a spitfire, one of those little women who could invoke fear in giants. One last glance in the mirror, ugh, and it was time to leave.

I grabbed my purse and keys from the nightstand, threw a jacket over my arm, not that I would need it, and headed for my car. Once inside, I sat there, going over the directions to her place in my head, and taking deep calming breaths. It was unbelievable how hard this was turning out to be. The nervous tremors in my arms and hands were so bad that it took me three attempts just to get the key into the ignition. One more deep breath, a tight grip on the steering wheel, and I was off. Just get it over with.

Eight

The drive to her house had taken longer than expected. I had underestimated traffic. It seemed all of Chicago was headed to her party. I finally made it to the parking lot across from her building. She rented the whole thing to prevent partygoers from having to incur the inflated parking rates. Four bucks an hour, insane! Already overwhelmed, I forced myself not to turn the car around and drive away. A large, red, white, and black banner plastered to the building that read 'Jazz's 20th B-Day Bash', even on a banner she refused to be called Jasmine.

I had almost forgotten how big Jazz made the last bash I had attended. Always determined to have the best parties and events, every event she planned was always coordinated with a matching name, theme, and color scheme. Every year she tried to outdo the last one. There were lights, streamers, and red and white flowers lining the walk and curb in front of the building. There was even a red carpet that covered the walkway that lead from the curb to the door. No way for a girl to pretend she was unable to find the place, say if she were trying to avoid social suicide.

REVITALIZED

I parked my car in the lot which was also decorated for the party with red and black flags all baring her initials. I ignored the line of cars waiting for the valet parking that she had apparently hired. I needed the extra time to prepare myself. I sat and stared at the flags which were classic Jazz, initials on the front and her profile outlined in black on the back. Ten minutes was enough procrastination. I hopped out of the car, double-checking to make sure the doors were locked, as if anyone would be tempted to steal my busted-up baby. There was a required guest book to sign which was manned by the 'bouncer', which was just her little cousin Mike who liked to work out a lot. I doubt he could have hurt anyone, who gave out rules of the party and directions to her apartment. It wasn't that complicated, get in elevator, press 12, and follow the decorations to party. Duh.

"Take the elevator to the top floor, and it's the last door on your right," he said as he checked my name off the list, not even glancing up from the clipboard. He was committed to his bouncer persona now, and if I hadn't known who he was, I totally would have bought it. As I walked away I wondered how many people had followed his directions and headed to the top floor only to have to be told the party was on the twelfth floor!

I stood in the elevator happy that I could catch an empty one, but being alone only helped make me even more nervous than I was before. I could hear the music before the doors even opened. I stepped off the elevator and followed the streamers, lights, and balloons; all in the same black and red color scheme, to the open double doors that led into her apartment. As I walked through the doorway my hands trembled. I gripped the strap of my purse tightly, and took another deep breath.

"Oh. My God!" The words rang out from across the room. I looked up to see my friend smiling and waving at me. Jazz ran over to me and wrapped her arms around me, hugging me so tightly that I thought she would break a rib.

"Hey Jazz," I struggled to pull my head back far enough to see her face. I would have hugged her back had she not pinned my arms to my sides with her bear hug.

She was short, I mean really, short, her head barely reached my shoulder. Her smile was wide and bright, and filled my heart with warmth just by looking at it. This was how I always felt around her. The only difference I could place was the color of her hair which was dyed to match the colors of the party. Her long locks, once blonde, were now a blazing mane of red that tickled my chin.

"You have no idea how happy I am that you actually came! I feel like you were my little sister, and you ran away from home," she kissed my cheek. "It's so good to have you back."

"Thanks," I sighed. She still referred to me as the younger sister, even though we were the same age,

70

"I can't honestly say that I was looking forward to this, but, now that I'm here, I'm glad I came… so far." I was finally able to wiggle my arms free, just enough to wrap them around her curvy frame. The girl was vertically challenged, but she had a body to die for.

Guilt rose from within me. Why? Well, possibly because I'd given up on myself, more times than I cared to count, but especially because of those last few days. There were other people in my life, maybe they were not blood, but they were my family. Had I wasted away alone, as I had hoped, decayed with time, my selfishness would have hurt them.

She grabbed my hand and pulled me around the room, introducing me to new faces and reintroducing me to the ones I was supposed to remember from high school (most of them barely remembered my name, feel the love). After about twenty minutes of her dragging me from person to person, I assured her that I would be fine on my own and told her to go off and enjoy her party. She didn't have to babysit me like I was some lost kid she'd found in the mall.

"Are you sure? I really don't mind, I'm just so happy you're here." She tried to encourage me, but it only made me feel worse.

"Jazz, I'm okay. I think I can manage walking around and having the occasional small talk without you holding my hand," I smiled at her, reassuring her that she wouldn't find me in the fetal position on the bathroom floor. I was a big girl, I could handle myself.

She nodded and with one more hug, reluctantly left my side. As she walked away, all of my comfort and confidence went with her. I stood there; frozen with everyone and everything around me moving at what seemed like hyper speed. I sunk into a corner with my back against the wall, and scanned the room with my eyes. There were so many people there; so many eyes. They all darted back and forth towards me. Even though I could barely hear over the music, I knew there was an influx of snickering and gossiping going on.

I tried to tell myself that they weren't talking about me, that I was the least important person at the party, and that it was paranoia getting to me. This night was all about Jazz, and that was the only reason everyone was here, not to gossip about me. I had almost gotten myself completely convinced when I overheard the group of girls next to me. A short, blonde standing to my left peered over her shoulder at me, she turned with the laugh of a horse, "Why did she even bother to come just to stand in the corner like some reject? Did she just escape from a mental clinic or something?"

Maybe, she assumed she was so far away that I wouldn't hear, or maybe she was just being a bitch. Whatever the reason was, it didn't stop it from hurting. I felt like I had been kicked in the gut. I wanted to run out of there, wanted to hide, to get away. I wasn't ready for this. Why did I let Jazz convince me to come? Of course, this was the perfect moment for my body to choose to betray me! I stood there, frozen, my eyes swelling with tears. My brain yelled commands that my limbs refused to follow. I took deep breaths pleading the tears not to spill over. I couldn't cry now, not in front of these people. In the past, I would have walked up to her and told her off, using words too complex for her bottle-blonde head to comprehend, but now, I just wanted to curl up into a ball and disappear. Years in solitude will take the gumption right out of you.

The warm affectionate crowd, the girls I once shared lunch, clothes, and stories of boys with, they were no more. The people I once knew were now cold, stuck up strangers, and I was no longer a part of their world. I begged my legs to move, but they still refused. My eyes scanned the crowd searching for Jazz's smile. If I could find her face, it would help me regain enough composure to be able to walk out of this place before the waterworks began, but I couldn't find her.

It was dark and there were way too many people jammed into the room now. I had completely forgotten about my early escape strategy, now I felt trapped; chained to the wall with no way out. I skimmed each section of the apartment trying to find something to focus on, something to calm me down, but there was nothing.

Panicked, my heart began to race, and my steady breathing turned into short gasps of air. This couldn't be happening, not here. I continued to try to find something; anything to stop the tears; knowing I wouldn't be able to hold them back much longer, and then I saw him.

He was standing directly across from me; I'm not sure how I could have missed seeing him before. His stormy gray eyes were focused on mine. Everything else was still moving way too fast, but he was still. His glare was intimidating, yet inviting. I looked away, trying not to stare, to find something else to focus on, but even my eyes were disobeying me. He was like a magnet, and if my body had been functioning properly, it would have crossed the room to get to him. When I looked back, he was still staring at me, but I avoided making eye contact and instead turned my attention to cataloging his features, committing them to memory.

He was tall at least six feet, maybe a few inches more. His hair thick and dark fell in waves that ended just below his shoulders. He wore black slacks, with a white fitted V-neck t-shirt. Winning the award for best dressed was clearly not a priority for him, and yet somehow, he was much more impressive than anyone else in the room.

His skin was smooth, without a hint of any blemishes (yes, I noticed, I was making a constant comparison to my own blotchy complexion, hello, self-conscious). I doubted that he ever had any run-ins with the evil known as acne, even while going through puberty, one of those lucky souls. I looked at his face. In a word, perfect, well at least in my opinion. Strong jaw line, deep set eyes, thick brow; it all came together as if someone had drawn him, measuring each feature so it fit his face flawlessly. His lips were thin and pink, a nice contrast against his five o'clock shadow, which should have looked messy, but on him, it looked intentional and added to his appeal. He looked like something out of a magazine, a page I could not turn. Not that I wanted to.

I noticed his breathing, the steady rise and fall of his chest and in moments my own calmed to match his. Every breath he took was another one for me. Nice and slow; even; steady. My eyes ran down his neck following the lines of his muscles to his chest and further still to the abs that teased me from beneath his thin white shirt.

The obnoxious little blonde next to me tripped and I looked down to make sure she was okay, and I claimed a small victory for myself. After watching her get up and dust off her dress, I locked back on him again; he was still staring at me and our eyes reconnected. His lips quivered with words he wanted to say or was trying not to.

I questioned if I had imagined it when I saw his hand slowly lift and hang in the air close to his body, as if he was reaching out to me. Like that super romantic moment in those Lifetime movies that was every girl's dream. I blinked a few times expecting the illusion to wipe away but it did not. He was still there, this handsome stranger, hand outstretched to me, I could swear I felt his fingertips on my skin caressing me with a low heat. My physical self was frozen solid, but there was something inside of me that was trying to get to him. It was like he was taking control of me, and I would be lying if I said I wanted him to stop.

The magnetic pull grew stronger, the affect not only touched my eyes but my entire body, every little bit of me was drawn to him. I wanted nothing more than to go to him, but my body had abandoned me. I was in an internal fight with the part of myself that had no name. I took a deep breath, imagining those breaths being strong enough to pull him to me, eliminating the need for my body to move.

"Oh, I see you've noticed Lacal," Jazz bounced up to my side smiling. "Yeah, he's a bit of a loner, but he is great to look at, so no one complains." She handed me a bottle of water.

Her voice ejected me from my trance. I gasped, taking in a deep breath, my chest burned as if I hadn't been breathing at all, as if I had been suffocating. My face surely told the story of my desire, but the tears had retreated, and were replaced by what felt like lava spreading over my entire body.

"Thanks," I grabbed the bottle of water from her, and turned to look at him again, I couldn't resist. The pull was intoxicating, and I wanted more, but he was gone. I searched for him through the crowd and found nothing.

"Girl, please don't worry yourself over him." Jazz interrupted my search. "That's just how he is. He's been coming around for months now, looking for someone, I think. He shows up from time to time like some spy, which of course is what most people have begun to call him. It is a bit of mystery. Each time, he pops in, makes little or no conversation, walks around, and then poof, he's gone again. I've learned to ignore him, well after I enjoy the view a little bit." She winked and laughed.

"What did you say his name was?" I couldn't get the image of him out of my mind. My breath was uneven; it seemed that when he had left he had taken my air with him as well.

"Lacal," she said no longer paying attention.

"Oh, um…look, I think I'm going to head home now." I handed her back the bottle.

"No, you can't go now!" she whined, looking disappointed. "Stay, please, it's been so long since you have been out with us, you can't leave just as the party's getting started."

"Look, Jazz, I'm just not that into this, and half the people here are not who I remember them to be, besides, I'm not feeling all that great." I sighed placing my hand on her shoulder. "We should get together soon, though. It's about time I stepped back into my life and who better to do that with than my best friend? Just, maybe not at a party?"

She smiled reluctantly, "Okay, well, I guess I should just be glad that you showed up. To be honest, I am surprised you came at all. I was ready to hear a bunch of excuses when I called you." She gave me a knowing look as if she could tell I had attempted to come up with one.

"We'll get together soon. I promise," I smiled at her, gave her a hug, and exited as fast as I could before she could think of any other reason for me to stay.

On the drive home, my only thought was him, Lacal. His name echoed in my mind. It just repeated over and over on an endless loop, the background music to my mental images of him. He stared at me and for a brief instant, damn near took over my body. All through a look! Did any of that really happen? Maybe, he was just a hallucination; created to help me through the disaster that was my return to the real world.

Jazz had seen him too. He was there, he was real, and his name was Lacal. I hadn't imagined him. I doubt that my imagination could ever be that good anyway. He was one of those guys that girls went gaga over, you just couldn't help it, and he was looking at me. No, more than looking, he was staring, and his eyes set my skin on fire. Either this was a perfect example of animal magnetism or I really had been home alone for far too long.

Once inside my garage, from the moment my feet hit the ground of the car, as corny as it sounds, I was floating. I dropped my bag on the kitchen table and sat in the chair next to it. My mind was on a remote island,

and of course I wasn't alone, Lacal, the gray eyed stranger was right there with me.

"Oh my god," I gasped, throwing my hand up in the air as the loudest clap of thunder just sounded off inside my head. You're sitting at the table! The internal voice screamed. The one place in my house that had been avoided; the disease riddled artifact of the past. Quickly retreating from the seat, my hands wave through the air as if they were burning from the contact. In hopes to escape, the chair was knocked over onto the floor as I ran out of the kitchen and up to my room.

Inside, the door slammed behind me. I was safe…. from the table. I tried every breathing technique and calming routine I could remember from my physical therapy, but nothing worked. I scrambled to the bathroom to get a glass of water. My hands shook so badly, I could barely lift the glass to my lips without spilling the water all over the floor.

I opened the medicine cabinet and grabbed for the bottle of Tylenol. The pounding in my head was so loud it was drowning out the sound of my thoughts. I wrestled with the cap; it flew off followed by a hand full of tablets that fell into the sink and down the drain. I poured some into my hand, I had no idea how many, and swallowed them down with the little water I could get into my mouth.

I stumbled back to my room, gasping for air. I couldn't take the pain anymore. I ran over to the nightstand that set next to my bed and pulled out the offensive green box. Inside was the vial that waited for me, glowing with invitation. Without a second thought, not even a moment of hesitation, I popped the fire shaped cork and poured the thick blue liquid down my throat.

It went down slow and icy leaving a stale taste behind, but it didn't matter, because within seconds I could breathe again. The world became fuzzy and hazy around the edges. Everything looked and felt soft. I flung myself across my bed and passed out as I landed on what felt like clouds plucked from the sky.

Nine

Heavy lids opened to the piercing sunlight that invaded my room through the window that was left uncovered. My body was stiff, and my back was cramped from the awkward position I had slept in. I sat up to stretch the kinks out of my body and as I extended my arms out and tightened my fists; I felt a stab in the palm of my hand. Blood trickled from the point of pain down my arm.

My eyes bulged as I watched the red drops hit the white blanket on the bed beside me. I opened my hand and there, crushed to pieces, was the vial my grandmother had left behind, and it was empty! I sat there confused, the decision to drink my grandmother's mystery concoction, may not have been the smartest thing I'd ever done, but then again, it was hard to remember even making the choice.

Still wearing the same clothes, I wore to Jazz's party, I could remember nothing else from the night before except the pain I had hoped to escape. In the bathroom I let the water run over my hand to clean the cut. Pieces of glass fell into the sink, clinking as they hit the ceramic frame. With each clink, a memory of the night before found its way back into my mind. My bouncy best friend, the overcrowded party, the pretentious people that I used to call friends; it all came back to me. There was something missing. I grabbed a towel and wrapped it around my hand before searching for the first aid kit in the cabinet under the sink.

Sitting on the tub, I was dumbfounded, not only about the missing pieces from last night, but from the apparent lack of pain in my hand. I saw the blood and the gash was clear of glass, but I felt nothing. Even as I poured peroxide on the cut, and watched it bubble as it hit the opening there was nothing. Sure, I could feel the coolness of the liquid, even the effect of the air that caused the fluid to bubble, but there was no pain. Maybe, I was just too tired, too out of it to process the feeling of pain. Not that it had ever happened before. Pain was pain and I always felt it. I finished cleaning up my hand and bandaged the cut.

As I cleaned up the mess, and wiped away the trickles of blood from the sink and the floor, I thought about the missing piece. That void in my memory of the party. Something was obviously out of place. I stood up again, tossing the tissues into the trash and looked at my face in the mirror. "Oh," I whispered. The face that reflected in the glass didn't resemble the one I'd become accustomed to. It was my face, but not the one that met me each morning when I dared a peek at my reflection

REVITALIZED

I looked completely different than before leaving my house last night. My face was fuller, and it actually had color again. My skin was clear. The blotches were gone. I looked like I was thriving, not at all like the sickly shell of a girl I'd become. I lifted my hand up to my face touching the space under my eyes. The darkness was gone; the telltale signs of sleepless nights. It looked as if I had just slept for weeks.

My eyes, the color was off. They no longer looked like they belonged to me. They were still hazel-brown, but now there were little bits of red flecks paired with the usual hints of green. I closed them tightly, assuming I was just exhausted, and my mind was playing tricks on me, wishful thinking backfiring. Of course, when I lifted my lids and caught my reflection again, the new me was still there with my new eyes.

Eyes...That was what I couldn't remember, those stormy gray intrusive eyes. Images of the mysterious guy returned to me riding in on a tidal wave of gray. I was back in that moment all over again.

"Lacal," it came out as a deep whisper from my lips, sounding animalistic, almost carnal, like pure instinct brought on by just the thought of him. My memory of him was now vivid. In sharp focus, there he was standing across the room from my paralyzed body. In a sea of busy bodies, everyone else rushing to make a scene, he was still, the only movement was the rise and fall of his chest, his breaths becoming my own. My body quivered with electric pulses as I remembered the feeling that took me over. I belonged to him.

My stomach warmed as if a roped of fire was tied around me, as if he had lassoed me and was trying to pull me into him. Lost in the memory, wrapped in the cloud of gray that reached out from his eyes, I was saddened by the realization that I would most likely never see him again. He was the random stranger, spying on the party full of beautiful women.

"Oh well," I sighed, concentrating once again on my new appearance to block out the images of him.

I looked down in the sink and saw the pieces of glass shimmering from the drain. They reminded me of the stale taste that the blue liquid had left in my mouth. I grabbed my toothbrush and scrubbed my mouth clean. It took two rounds of brushing and three hits of mouthwash to remove the taste of metal from my mouth.

Nana's miracle cure had actually worked! She had been right all along. I felt one hundred percent better. For the first time in nearly three years, there was no pain, no spasms, no physical reminder of how broken I had been. My grandmother hadn't been delusional as my mother suggested. I smiled at the reminder of both their faces and wished they could see me, fully restored. My mother wouldn't be pleased about how it happened, but I knew that she would be happy to see me better, what parent wouldn't be?

REVITALIZED

I went to my room, and stood in front of the full-length mirror to better study myself. Overnight, it seemed that I had made a full transition. My favorite outfit which I was still wearing actually fit me again, instead of hanging from my frame like it would a mannequin. I had my curves back. Not the sensual, Latin ones my best friend had claim on, but my thighs, hips and butt had returned to their glory days, back when I was a runner. As I turned in the mirror; I found it difficult to believe the changes I saw. Everything was firm and plump, and my skin was glowing. I flexed my legs and arms and stretched my muscles while I waited for the pain to return. It never did.

It was a thing of awe; I revisited the possibility of this all being a dream; that would make more sense, more logical than a magic cure. Even if it wasn't real, it still felt amazing, even if it was just a figment of my imagination. I sighed when I heard my phone ringing. That had to be the signal that it was time to wake up.

I stood there waiting for the inevitable shock that would drag me from my dream back into reality, but it never came, and the phone just kept ringing. I looked over my shoulder by the bed at the cordless phone on my nightstand. The phone continued to ring but the fantasy never released me from its grips. It wasn't really possible for any of this to be real. Once I woke up, it would be torture. I looked at myself one last time, wishing I had the chance to at least take my new body for a test drive.

The ringing stopped, but resumed just a few moments later. I walked over to my bed. Maybe this was a part of the dream that I had to go along with. I picked the phone up and pressed the call button to answer.

"Hello?" I hesitated before speaking, I had to figure out what kind of dream this was. If it was a nightmare, something was sure to jump out of the phone and attack me.

"Hey, so you are awake. Are you okay?" Jazz's voice came through the receiver. "I tried calling your cell phone, but it went straight to voicemail."

"Yeah, I guess I am," I still was not convinced that I wasn't dreaming. "I think I left my cell downstairs or in the car maybe. I'm not really sure."

"Uh…okay, so are you feeling any better?"

"Huh?"

There was a pause before she spoke, the silent signal of her suspicions kicking in. "You left early last night. You said you weren't feeling up to staying at the party."

"Oh, yeah I'm fine…actually I feel pretty good today." I flexed my fingers expecting the pain from the cut to set in. Maybe I was awake, but how?

"Well, I'm glad to hear that, because I am coming to get you. I need to do a bit of summer shopping and apparently so do you judging from that frock of a shirt you were wearing last night. I'll be there in an hour," she hung up, once again not giving me anytime to formulate an excuse to get out of going. She had gotten better at setting traps for me. I made a mental note to work on my reflex times. I used to be so good at dodging her set ups.

"Here we go again." I sighed and laughed at her underhanded jab at my wardrobe. Yep, she was the same Jazz she'd always been.

I went to my closet and pulled out a pair of jeans and a tank top, simple and comfortable, Jazz would hate it. I hopped in the shower and washed up as quickly as I could while simultaneously trying not to get the bandage on my hand wet. Once dressed, I pulled my hair up in a ponytail, and looked at myself in the mirror, this time a lot less intently. Secretly, I accepted my new look and hoped to God that it would last. I feared that if I said it out loud, it would all be taken away.

This was amazing; the idea that I had a second chance at life. Solemnly, I wondered if there was any way to make it stick. Could this only be a temporary fix? I didn't want to get too accustomed to this face and body, but I was going to try and enjoy it while I had the chance.

Jazz showed up exactly one hour later, she was always on time. I walked to her car trying to subdue the anxiety that was beginning to build. Would she notice the changes in my appearance? How could she not? There weren't just a few minor revisions; I had developed an entirely different body overnight. Before I could finish questioning what her reaction would be, her face revealed the answer.

"Oh my god," her mouth fell open. "Whatever you took, I want some now!"

Jazz sat by the curb in her new fire red Porsche Boxter, another birthday gift from her father. The car matched her hair, which I could see was fire engine red and the same as Rihanna's whose song Hard was blasting from the car stereo. I couldn't remember if it had been that shade of red last night or if it was a new addition to her image. Jazz had been known to change hair color overnight to match a new outfit like a chameleon.

The car, though a bit loud in color choice, was perfect for her. It was small, but not to be underestimated. I could see that Jazz was proud of her choice by the way she beamed as I walked up. Her first car was a Porsche as well, it was much older and not half as nice as this one, but it was enough to make her swear that she would never drive any other make of car no matter how out of place it made her look.

"A good night's' sleep and warm tea," I told the obvious lie and attempted to shrug it off. I could only hope that she wouldn't press for a real answer. Not that the truth sounded any more believable.

"*Right*," the word was sarcastically stretched out to make it clear that she did not believe me. She eyed the bandages on my palm, "What happened to your hand?"

"Chopping fruit, you remember how uncoordinated my hands are." Of course, I couldn't tell her the truth. She smiled seeming to believe that one, no one who really knew me would ever doubt my ability to injure myself.

"Yeah, well let's go." I heard the laughter she tried to stifle as I walked around the car to the passenger door.

Ten

We went to the Chicago Ridge Mall, which was apparently still Jazz's favorite place to shop. As innovative as she was with her wardrobe, she was surprisingly indifferent to changes in her everyday life. I wondered when they had installed the Merry-go-round in the middle of the food court, and if it was even necessary, but I kept the comment to myself. I didn't want to bring attention to the fact that I had not been to the mall in years. No one paid any attention to the carousel and the one time they turned it on, there were only three people on it, each of them holding babies too small to enjoy the ride. Jazz said she loved it, and tried but failed, to get me to take a ride with her.

Shopping with Jazz wasn't at all what I remembered it to be. While she was interested in examining every item she laid her hand on to make sure each detail would flatter her figure, I was fighting the urge to dash out of every store like it was about to catch fire. She had effectively turned me into the impatient, embarrassed boyfriend, forced to carry around his girlfriend's purse, while reading the annoying girly magazines outside the dressing room. I had to judge at least five outfits in each store. After a while, they all started to look the same to me. I was sure at some point in my life I was able to enjoy this, perhaps just as much as Jazz did, but I could not for the life in me remember why.

Jazz could tell that I wasn't enjoying our outing as much as she wanted me to. She made every effort to make it more entertaining for me, even going to the lengths of putting together outfits for me which she then had me model for her. Yeah, that only made the experience worse. It made me feel more self-conscious. Even though I had this new magical new body, my mind was still reacting the way it had after I looked at myself the night before going to her party. I still felt the need to calculate every move and turn, comparing myself to the other people there. Yes, there was my new reflection, but in my head, I was still that sickly, blotchy skinned, underweight girl.

After three long hours spent between four different stores, Jazz decided it was time to take a break and get some food. I couldn't have been more relieved. While I had picked out two shirts and one pair of pants during the excursion, Jazz had four bags stuffed with new outfits.

"You're such a light weight now, you know that?" Jazz laughed as we sat down with our pizza slices.

"Yeah, I haven't made much time for shopping in a while," I tossed a weak smile her way.

"So, is there something on your mind? You seemed a little preoccupied today," she took a sip of her drink peering at me over the brown sunglasses she wore.

"Um…" I took a moment to question whether or not to tell her about the thoughts of the strange new guy I met at her party that I could not get out of my head. Staring at this small girl, eager to rekindle our friendship, I gave in. "Yeah, actually, I was wondering about that Lacal guy. I can't get him off my mind." As the words left my mouth I instantly regretted saying anything.

"Oh, so that's what this is about?" She looked at me condemningly, yet I could tell she was enjoying the chance for gossip.

"What, what is about?" I took a bite of pizza giving me an excuse to look away.

"You know the zombie-like state you have been in for the last few hours. I was beginning to think I had lost my best shopping buddy," she wiped her forehead and flung the imaginary sweat away.

"Oh," I couldn't bring myself to tell her that I just wasn't as into the circus of shopping anymore, "Yeah, I guess I was thinking about him more than I thought."

"Well, like I said before, don't waste your time girl. He is basically a ghost," she took a big bite of pizza and rolled her eyes.

"So, no one knows anything about him?" I hoped the disappointment didn't show too much on my face.

"Nope," she sipped her drink, "I mean, I asked around about him when he first started showing up around town. You know I get that nosiness from my mother, but I got nowhere. No one seems to know him. I'm not even sure how he got into my party last night. He wasn't on the guest list, but then again, he never is." She frowned; clearly disappointed that she hadn't been able to find any dirt on this new mystery man.

"That's too bad." I wanted to find out more, but with Jazz it was best to leave it alone. She would turn it into a big deal if I continued to dig for info. Maybe even launch a massive search party to find him. I wouldn't put it past her. Count me out of the inquisition.

"You two would make a cute couple though," she attempted to keep the topic alive, maybe to keep me from slipping back into my 'zombie' frame of mind.

"Ha, you think?" I grimaced at the thought of what we would look like together, in my mind I looked dull and lifeless against his glow. He was regal, polished and I was more than a little rough around the edges even with my new body. He was a rare breed, the type of guy that only exists in movies and fairytales.

"Yeah, and I saw the way he was looking at you," she paused pretending to fan herself with her hand, "clearly, he was interested in more than where you got your shoes from."

She peered over the edge of the table, looked at my feet, and frowned. She didn't attempt to hide the fact that she was disappointed by the beat-up sneakers I had on. I pulled my feet out of view and tucked them underneath my chair.

"It was pretty intense, but he couldn't have been that interested, he didn't even bother to say hi," I refused to get too excited about the situation. I decided to downplay it. I figured that if I didn't get my hopes up, there wouldn't be as big of a letdown if I never saw him again.

"Yeah, I guess, but I'm telling you, he never gave anyone the time of day before you. I mean girls would be lined up for days to get his attention, just to get a glance from him, and something tells me he wanted to give you much more than that." She laughed aloud and then coughed as if she was choking. Her eyes widened, and I would have sworn she was seeing the walking dead.

"What is it?" I turned to see what she was so shocked about and almost choked on the bite of pizza I had just taken.

"Oh. My. God." Jazz was now shaking my arm, completely unaware that I was already conscious of what she had been gawking at.

"What is he doing here? I thought you said he was like a ghost or something," the pull engaged again, making me feel both self-conscious and excited. Standing across the food court, scanning the crowd with his eyes, was the same guy from the party; Lacal, looking classic in a simple pair of black jeans and a white polo shirt.

"I've never seen him here," she looked at him and then back at me. "This is so freaky, I mean we were just talking about him; maybe it's a sign that we should go talk to him." Her eyes widened again this time with more thrill rather than shock.

"Are you crazy?" I could not believe what she had suggested. Without giving me time to protest, she grabbed my arm and dragged me through the crowd. "Don't do this Jazz; this is going to be really awkward." I whined pulling back with very little effort, of course part of me was excited about being near him again.

"Oh, come on!" She stopped for a moment, stared me in the eye, and then continued her pursuit. "Besides, you know you want the chance to be properly introduced to him. What better person to do that than me?" She snickered as she closed in on her target.

I couldn't disagree; I couldn't even stop my legs from moving. Each step that brought me closer to him only intensified that pull I felt coming from him. Even if I wanted to fight it, there was no way my body would allow it. I looked at him; his eyes were still examining the room. He was gorgeous. My heart started to beat so loud that at one point, it was all I could hear.

"Hey, Lacal!" Jazz was waving her hands and shouting across the room as if they were old friends; I dropped my head, mortified. Sometimes Jazz could be so embarrassing, sure we would laugh about it later, but at that moment I just wanted to hide.

He turned to see us barreling towards him. The muscles in his face twitched as he tried to prevent a smile. The brief glint of excitement in his eyes, was quickly replaced by indifference. He nodded his head at us once and then looked away. My heart dropped like a cannonball launched into the sea, it smashed into the depths of my stomach. Had I imagined that entire scene at the party? Could I have been so desperate for a way out of that awkward situation that I had created an imaginary connection between us?

"Hi Lacal, I want to introduce you to someone," Jazz said as she tugged me closer to her side when we reached him standing by the glass doors that led out to the parking lot. For a split second, I thought of dashing through them and racing toward the car, but that would be absolutely pointless since Jazz had driven. "This is my friend, Alexa. Alexa, this is Lacal." She pushed me closer to him.

"Uh, hi," I gave a weak smile and looked away, before I became lost in his eyes. I remembered how it felt, the cloud of gray that filled my mind. If I let that happen again, I really would become a zombie.

"Hello," he stuck his hand out to shake mine. The heaviness of my hand prevented me from reciprocating. In fact the entire arm felt numb, like an implant that didn't belong to me. Jazz grabbed my hand and shoved it into his. He shook my hand slightly and then dropped it. I must have had a comical expression on my face, because he looked as if he was fighting back laughter. I bit my lip and tried as best as I could not to blush, but lost the battle when Jazz started to giggle.

"Well, I have to go," Jazz blurted out and I turned to see her face and tried to ignore the weird twinges that were happening in the pit of my stomach. She was up to something and whatever it was, something that wouldn't make me happy.

"What?" If looks could cut, Jazz's face would have bled beneath my glare.

"Yeah, I have an, um, appointment that I completely forgot about. Lacal, you wouldn't mind giving Lex here a ride home, would you?" Before either of us could respond, she was running away and waving at us behind her. I was stuck there, looking at her bouncy, red hair as she disappeared into the crowd. Even after she was gone, I couldn't turn around. I could tell he was still there, his eyes burned holes into my back.

How could she do this to me?! Jazz had always been sneaky, but this was just low down! I'd barely been out of my house for two years, and now I was stuck here, the mall of all places, with this magnetic guy with the gray eyes the threatened to capture me. On top of that, I was stuck accepting a ride home with him, because she just ran away. I just knew I would find a way to embarrass myself. By the time I could make it to the parking lot and remember where the car had been parked, she would be long gone. I had to come up with an escape plan. There just had to be a way out of this, maybe I could take the bus, it would only take me about three hours to get home, if I didn't miss the next one, then I would have to wait an additional hour. Just great! Jazz was really going to hear it for pulling this one.

"Are you okay?" His voice broke through my scheming like liquid heat. It flowed through me sending every nerve on a rampage. I turned slowly to face him and tried to keep my heart rate even. How could he have gotten me so worked up with three little words? Just hearing his voice, I wanted to jump him right there in the middle of the crowded mall. Just imagine the pictures. They were sure to go viral!

"Um…yes I am okay." I met his eyes reluctantly with a shy grin. "I'm sorry; I can't believe she just did that." I shook my head, an attempt to regain some of the composure I had lost.

"Yeah," he stopped to clear his voice as if assessing how to go forward, "Good thing I actually have a car, or this would be very inconvenient for you." He smiled a wide grin that stretched from ear to ear. A Kool-Aid smile as my dad would call it. It made me want to laugh but I didn't. His teeth were perfect and luminous, surrounded by those thin lips that I so wanted to kiss.

"You don't have to give me a ride, I'm sure I can find someone else to pick me up," a lie, there was no one else, but I didn't want him to feel obligated. "Or I can just grab a cab."

"No, it's fine, I really don't mind." He looked away for a moment before returning his gaze to me, waiting for a response. "If it's okay with you."

"I just don't want to make you go out of your way," I said looking down at my hands. I wondered how we must have looked to everyone else. Shy, uncomfortable, maybe they would think we were on a first date. There's that wishful thinking again!

"I insist on taking you home. I don't think Jasmine would be very happy if I didn't. After all, she is very strong willed, and I wouldn't want to get on her bad side," he spoke smoothly. I wondered if it was his upbringing or if he was nervous as well, you know, like when you are on a job interview. I could not remember the last time I anyone called Jazz by her full name. If she would have heard him, she would have attempted to claw his eyes out. "Did you want to go home right away?"

His question caught me off guard. I assumed he would want to get this over as quickly as possible, but his eyes told of more, of anticipation. He hoped I would say no, that I would accept his offer of extending my time away from home. Honestly, I didn't want to go home, not yet anyway, not if I had a chance to spend any time with him. I took in his expression, and tried to decipher what my response should be. Outside of his eyes, he was a blank canvas. What if I had misread the meaning behind the look? Maybe he was just hungry or smelled something bad.

The problem was that I couldn't be sure if, or when, I might see him again; Jazz had referred to him as a spy. What if this was my only chance to get to know him? I needed to figure out what this attraction was that I had toward him. If what Jazz said was true, he would disappear again, and I would never see him again. Not unless I attended every one of Jazz's parties with her uppity friends, no thank you. Those parties were to be avoided like the plague! I thought about how to respond without sounding desperate.

"Well, I don't want to interfere with any of your plans. I'm just along for the ride now," I figured the best way to find out what he really wanted was to put the ball back in his court. Girl handbook 101 strikes again! I looked off past him to appear as if it didn't matter either way to me.

"Are you sure? I don't mind, I can understand how awkward this might be for you," using my own move against me. The ball was back in my court. Great!

"Um...yea, I've been cooped up at home for too long. It's nice to be back out into the world. Even if it isn't exactly what I had planned for the day." I gave a small smile, the smallest I could manage. The key was not to seem too eager.

"So, to get away from being cooped up in the house, you go to the mall? If you don't mind, maybe I can take you somewhere more appropriate for what you're trying to accomplish," he smiled at me, directly at me with eye contact, and I nearly fainted! He could take me anywhere he wanted, no problem.

"More appropriate, what do you mean?" Surprisingly my brain was still able to form coherent thoughts because my body felt like mush.

"Yes. When you're trying to get out of the house, you need to get out into nature, not just transfer to another building." He reached out, grabbed my hand, and pulled me behind him leading the way out the doors and into the parking lot. I would have resisted, just for show, but the feel of his skin was electric. My body followed him willingly, wanting to experience more of him.

"Aah…nature, I think I remember what that is," I laughed, trying to cover the embarrassing flush of red that filled my cheeks. The warmth of his hand against my skin felt unreal. Of course this was not the first time I had held hands with a guy, but this was different, the way our hands fit perfectly together, it was like we were touching, not holding hands at all, like through a simple touch we had become one. The sensation was simply incredible. I had never met a guy who was this intoxicating to me before. Even my biggest crush,

Miguel, the guy with the legs of a dancer, hadn't remotely come close to this level of intensity.

We walked to the black car that waited in the parking lot. Just like him, it was uncomplicated and yet it seemed out of place. It was a Cadillac CTS; I remembered seeing it in a commercial. I stopped for a moment to admire it. I would have been embarrassed to have my car parked anywhere near it. I thought of the little sedan that sat in my garage covered in dirt and begging for the loving touch or maintenance. First, Jazz's brand new Porsche and now this. Was someone trying to tell me something?

"Are you coming?" Lacal stood looking at me, his eyes wide with pride, happy that I had recognized how kickass his car was. The way his chest puffed up reminded me of a kid showing off a new toy.

"Yeah, um…nice car," I tried to keep it simple and hoped he didn't go into that car talk most guys did. Rambling on about engines, motors, and other whatnots I could never really understand. I could name a few makes and models, but that was pretty much as far as my car knowledge went, (if didn't see it on T.V. in a commercial, I didn't know it) which was a contributing factor to the sad condition of my own ride.

"Thanks." He held the passenger door open for me. I got in stiffly but felt relief, so maybe he wasn't a car buff; maybe he just owned a nice car.

Butterflies fluttered wildly in my stomach, just like they had when I was 14 and on my first date. The one my mother protested, and my father was only too happy to see happen. Go figure! My mom claimed my dad's enthusiasm was because he liked the boy. He was 15 years old, a star basketball player, and already being scouted by the NBA. My dad had high hopes for this young athletic power couple. So what if later I would turn on the television and watch as he accepted an MVP award. I could only imagine the look of disappointment on my father's face now. Hell, Alexa Rose does have a ring to it.

My palms started to sweat, a sign of an oncoming panic attack. The calming techniques I'd learned were engaged to quickly deter it as he walked around to the driver side. Inside, the car was spotless which did not help my anxiety. I pulled my arms in tight against my body. I didn't want to touch anything, knowing how clumsy I was, I would probably break something. He got in the car and stopped to stare at me before putting the key in the ignition.

"What's wrong? Do you need to go home?" It took me a moment to realize how I must have looked to him. Bottled up into myself, he probably thought I was in pain. I loosened my arms and tried to appear more relaxed.

"No, I'm fine, so where are we going?" Though I altered my demeanor, he still looked at me with a puzzled expression.

"I thought we would go to a park. Maybe get some fresh air into your lungs," he smiled at me and started the car.

The beginning of our ride was taken in silence. It would've been nice to strike up a conversation, but my nerves had my voice in a chokehold. It he hadn't seemed preoccupied with his own thoughts, perhaps he could have started the chatter. There was an odd familiarity in his posture as he drove with one arm perched up on his knee with his fist under his chin. The Thinker. Almost recognizable, but from a different time. I'd only seen him once before and we hadn't even spoken to each other that time. I began to wonder where this park was, when he pulled over for a pit stop at Wal-Mart. I don't know why this was a comforting sign. Maybe it was because it made me feel like he was not like the people at Jazz's party who wouldn't be caught dead within 50 feet of this place.

I was asked to wait in the car, so I did. He refused to let me know what he had purchased declaring it a surprise. He could always be informed at a later time about my extreme distaste for surprises! Patience was a virtue that this girl was in short supply of. If you tell me you have a surprise for me I go completely nuts, but then he smiled at me, my heart melted, my blood boiled and I completely forgot about how much I disliked his announcement.

"I hope you don't mind the drive," he looked over to me and smiled again. How could I say no?

"Not at all," I smiled, maybe a little too wide and tried to recover, "like I said, it's been awhile since I was out of the house for more than just grocery shopping."

"Why is that?" He asked focusing on the road ahead.

"I was pretty sick for a while," I balled my fist, thinking of the pain that used to take over my body and the pain that should have been there after having pulled shards of glass from my hand just that morning. What was going on beneath the bandage? Had the wound completely healed? That was impossible.

It was unbelievable how great it felt to be with Lacal, for a while, my fear of waking up from this dream where miracle cures and hot guys existed was forgotten. His presence made it easier to accept this as my new reality; the changes were a lot less unsettling. I listened again for my alarm clock or my cell phone to sound off and yank me out of this fairy tale story come to life. The pain would inevitably return, and my life would go on numbingly, just as it had before I drank the liquid metal.

The real me was probably laid across my bed with a smile plastered across her face. I hope she was enjoying every bit of this illusion. If all of this was some elaborate creation of my mind, let me sleep forever. This new life was so much better than what would come with the return to consciousness; even if it was just a fantasy, it was totally worth it. Jazz was still in my corner and that made me happier than I'd been in a long time. On top of getting my best friend back, being here with Lacal felt so right and comforting. As nervous as he made me feel, I couldn't fathom the idea that he was a figment of my imagination. I wanted to know everything about him; I couldn't wake up before I got the chance.

For all I knew, the clock was running out and I had to spend every moment absorbing as much of him as humanly possible. Maybe if I knew more about him it would make it easier to leave him behind in this dream world, or perhaps it would only torture me more. The knot forming in my stomach told me nothing would be enough if I wasn't able to keep him.

Eleven

"Are you okay?" He asked apprehensively. His brow wrinkled with anxiety and worry.

The car was now stopped next to a quaint little park. The first thing I noticed was all the trees, mostly Weeping Willows; they had always been my favorite because of the way their branches hung and swayed in the wind. To me they were the free spirits of the trees. Just outside the window was a small path that led to a little pond, surrounded by beautiful smooth blue rocks and pebbles that sprinkled out into the grassy hill beyond it.

The place was underrated in its beauty. As simple as it was, it still took my breath away. I tried to memorize it just in case I never got another chance to take it all in. Even now, I couldn't tell you where we were, I was too wrapped up in trying to look normal during the drive to pay attention to the street signs. Gee, smart move for a girl alone in a car with a strange guy. Yes, he was attractive, but pretty people can be deranged too. Somehow, I would find a way to ask about his intentions without sounding paranoid that he would hurt me.

"I'm fine, sorry, I got lost in thought." I smiled at him reassuringly. "So, this is what qualifies as a more appropriate place for me to go to get out of the house?"

"Yes, it is," he smiled, washing the concern from his eyes. "Do you like it? I come here from time to time just to get away from the madness of the world." Smiling, he touched my hand, and then climbed out of the car. He stood just outside the door, spread his arms out wide, and said, "Welcome to my own little piece of paradise."

Taking that as an invitation to join him, I stepped out of the car. He led me to a little white fence sitting just besides a rock path that led through the grass. As we walked, I inhaled deeply, filling my lungs and enjoying the scent of freshly cut grass, blended with newly blossomed wild flowers. He was right; I needed to be in nature, simply being outside with the breeze moving across my skin, it felt like *home*.

We sat on the edge of a large bolder when we reached the pond. Lacal was just as enchanted by our surroundings as I was. He looked even more amazing in the sun. The light bounced off his skin as he held his eyes closed with his head tilted toward the sky soaking up the warmth of the rays.

"So," he sighed, "please tell me you are enjoying this." He didn't look at me as he spoke, but there was a slight lift at the corner of his lips, a smile.

"Yes, I really am." Pulling the strands of hair away from my face and tightening my ponytail, I closed my eyes and let the warmth of the sun melt away any anxieties I had about losing him.

"Good," his hand slid over the stone to touch mine and I opened my eyes to see him now staring out at the water. There was a fight happening inside of him, one that I could see on his face, but could not bring myself to ask about. Unable to look away, I watched and waited for his struggle to be over. The pause stretched longer, but never felt uncomfortable. "You look different now."

It never occurred to me that he would notice the changes in my appearance. I was barely able to brush the subject aside with Jazz, how was I supposed to avoid it with him when there were no distractions. I thought for a moment and tried to come up with an explanation that didn't make me seem like a total nut job, but once again found myself defunct.

"Yeah," I pulled my hand away from his, and began twisting my fingers together. Maybe, if I just left it at that, he would too.

"So, what happened?" He looked at me intently. Just like Jazz, he didn't know when to let a subject go.

"I can't explain it." I decided to be as honest as I could without saying anything that would send him running for the hills. "Like I said, I was sick for a while. You saw me yesterday, my appearance was, um,

109

lacking. Up until this morning, that is how I always looked."

"What changed?" He still did not look at me, more for my benefit than his.

"My grandmother, she was pretty into spiritual things, what some people might refer to as 'magic'," I paused to see how he was taking the information. He didn't make any odd expressions, indicating that he may have been concerned about my sanity. He didn't scoot away or suggest we end our little impromptu date, so I decided it was safe to continue. "My grandmother had tried to get my mother to let her help me, but my mother refused it; she said she would never allow me to be a part of that lifestyle, she felt it went against nature. I followed my mother's wishes and did as she asked, but the pain was becoming too much for me to handle. It sucks to admit it, but I was desperate for any kind of relief. I barely remember taking it, but I can only assume that I did, because, well look at me."

"Why would your mother refuse?" He looked as if he couldn't understand why anyone would have an aversion to trying anything that could help her daughter.

"Well, I never really understood that either. She called it 'black magic' and actually restricted me from visiting my grandmother after I became ill. I wasn't allowed to be alone with her. I just figured my mother was superstitious and never gave it a second thought," It hurt to think of my mother and grandmother and of all the time that I had lost with them both. Time that I could never get back.

"So now that you have gone against her wishes, how is she taking it?" He picked up a small pebble and flicked it out onto the water, skipping it five times before it sunk to the bottom.

"She's not," I paused as my eyes began to fill with tears, but I was unable to restrain them. "My mother and father both disappeared over a year ago." I couldn't say that she had died, although they were declared legally dead after the search was called off, but it was easier to think that they were just lost. They were alive somewhere, just not with me.

"Disappeared?" He leaned turning his face towards mine; I could feel his silent attempt to urge me to continue.

"Yes, well something like that, their car was found on the side of a road somewhere in Iowa, but they weren't in it. The police could only come up with one explanation, though they never proved their theory." I paused trying harder to prevent the tears.

"What was the theory?"

"They assumed that the car was stolen. As far as my parents were concerned, I decided not to listen. They never found them; there was no trace of them having ever even been in the car. At first, I was able to convince myself that they were somewhere safe and happy, and that they just chose to run away. After a while, the idea of my parents simply choosing to leave me behind hurt

111

more than anything else." I couldn't hold them back any longer; the salty rivulets spewed past my lids and fell down my face. I dropped my head attempting to hide them from him.

He lifted my face back to his with his and stared at me for a moment. He watched as the tears fell and bit his lip, struggling again with words he was unsure of. He lifted his finger and wiped away my tears before putting it to his lips. The moisture glistened against his pink flesh.

"I'm sorry; I didn't mean to make you cry," his face had moved in to mine. We were so close, it was that frightening amount of intimacy that threatened to rip me open and reveal all my innermost secrets. Ones I myself didn't know were there.

"No, its fine. I've been blocking out these feelings for so long, I guess it was time to let them out, I just wish I hadn't ruined everything by crying." He touched a falling tear with his thumb and rubbed it across my lips leaving them with the taste of salt.

He held my head to his, pressing our foreheads together, his breath tickled my lips leaving tiny sparks that landed on my skin threatening to ignite my flesh. His eyes widened with intensity as he took a deep breath and bit his lip. He was holding back, and I hoped he'd lose control. I was captivated again and happily drowning in the deep ocean of gray that stared back at me. Breathing became harder to manage; preoccupied with trying to use my mind to will him to kiss me, much like I had done at the party. His jaw tensed, and he held my face firmly between his hands, his thumb stroking my cheek. I screamed inside my head for him to end my agony and allow me to taste him. His lips, moistened by his tongue, parted slightly, his breath now ragged like my own. I bit my lip in anticipation. He leaned in closer; finally! I closed my eyes, to concentrate on stopping the tremor of my lips. Kissing him was one time my awkwardness would not be acceptable.

I felt his lips, warm and soft, pressing against my right eye, and then my left, with soft peaks, like feathers brushing across my skin. I took a deep breath using the action to move myself closer to his lips without appearing to do so.

The electrical pulses that were traveling across my body were too much for me to take. Each one ended its journey on my lips, building like embers of a flame. He had to kiss me and extinguish the burn, or I would explode. The closer I got to him, the faster they raced through me. I took a deep breath; preparing my body for the jolt that I would feel when our lips finally met. I waited for the explosion, but it never came.

"Are you ready for your surprise?" His voice was now further away; his breath no longer teasing my lips.

I opened my eyes to see him sitting across from me, on his own side of the stone, his face full of contentment once again. He seemed calm and unaffected, but my body still strummed in anticipation. I wanted him to kiss me, to let me swim in the gray again and never come out. I wanted to feel his skin against mine and hold him there forever.

He seemed to be over it, the moment that nearly set me aflame, so I told myself to let it go. I couldn't let my mind get my body too excited or I would never be able to concentrate on getting through the rest of the day. I managed a tight nod before he turned away to walk back to the car.

#

Watching his figure disappear around the willow tree took me back to the night I tried never to think about. My mother smiled at me before she left with my dad. They were going to a party which was being held in her honor to celebrate her achievements with her volunteer services. She was a pillar of the community and it made me proud to be her daughter. I wanted to be there to support her, but the pain was too intense that night. It was one of the worst attacks my body had suffered, nearly as bad as the first one. Summoning the strength to walk them to the door had me near tears, but I had to do it. I had to show her as much support as I could. The moment the door closed behind them, my body would collapse to the sofa.

She looked beautiful. Because I couldn't go with them, she let me spend the evening watching her as she got dressed instead of urging me to rest like she normally would. It was a visual tease, an example of the life I should have been living. In college with my friends, getting dressed up for parties and events. I should have been enjoying life. Instead, my enjoyment came from watching others live. Eventually, I would begin to resent them for it. I was alone, but I didn't complain, not out loud anyway. It was my choice to push everyone away. The blame for my state of loneliness rested on my shoulders alone.

The most contact I had with the outside world came in form of the mailman. He would stop in and talk to me for a few minutes every day because he knew my situation and felt sorry for me. Even though she would never admit it, these visits started because of my mother. As much as she wanted to be brave and believe that somehow everything would be okay, she worried about me and my safety. Some days she had to leave me, this was her way of checking in on me without making me feel like a child who couldn't take care of herself.

My father waited for her at the foot of the stairs. When he saw her, he looked like a kid again, a boy picking up his date for the prom. His eyes lit up in that way that only told of one thing, love. The way she blushed in return made me hope that someday there was a love like that waiting for me. Even after nearly 20 years of marriage, they were still very deeply in love. What girl wouldn't want that?

Whenever they came to mind there were the same voices in my head that shouted at me, they scolded me about how foolish it was to let them out of my sight. Those precious last moments could have been so much more. We should have kissed and hugged each other; I

116

should have told them how much they meant to me and how much I loved them. None of that happened. A simple wave, a 'See ya later', and they were gone.

The wind picked up, its assault shocked me back to the present and passed a chill through my body. I rubbed my arms with the palms of my hands wishing my sleeves were longer. I turned at the sound of footsteps approaching from behind; Lacal was walking up with a large basket in his hand and two blankets draped over his arm.

"A picnic?" I stood to follow him as he walked to the patch of grass across from where we sat on the stone by the pond.

"Yes, well, I noticed you didn't finish your food back at the mall; I thought this would be appropriate. I wasn't sure what you would like so I got fruits and vegetables. They came together on a platter with some meats and cheeses. I also got some crackers to go along with them." So he had been watching us, how else would he have known about my half eaten pizza left sitting on my tray? He smiled proud of his selection. I couldn't bring myself to tell him I didn't eat pork and therefore half the food would be untouchable. At least the crackers were free of pork juice.

Sitting on the blanket he laid out, I watched as he pulled items out of the basket and arranged them between us. As he moved, the muscles in his arms flexed and revealed themselves. Had I been assessing his physical stature, this would have given me a sense of security. If there ever was something that caused me to need physical protection, he would be able to handle it. Good thing I wasn't making any assessments!

The sweetness of his actions oddly felt wasted on me. My generation of woman was taught to rally against this kind of display. We were supposed to be independent, and most men were welcoming the idea of an international assassination of chivalry. Lacal, however, didn't seem to be one of those men. I wasn't sure how I felt about that, my mom always told me to be strong and independent, but my dad spoiled me behind her back. Talk about giving a kid mixed messages!

"Are you okay?" His voice pulled me from my thoughts and once again, I was locked inside of him. The magnetism was still there, I was waiting for it to lose its intensity, for the attraction to fade. With extended time together, the thrill of the mystery man should have lessened, but instead it seemed to be growing. Each time looked at him it was harder to stay planted. My body begged for me to move closer to him.

"Yeah lost inside my head again, sorry," I had to get used to having conversations with other people again, and shut off the ongoing commentary that usually played in my mind to keep me company.

"I got orange or apple juice," when he didn't get a response he dug in the basket for another bottle. "There is always water."

"Apple is fine, thank you." If this continued, he would probably think I had some form of mental disorder, slipping into my own little world every time there was a lull in the conversation.

He handed me a plastic cup and poured juice into it before pouring some for himself.

"This is nice. I didn't think people still did stuff like this," my generic comment was meant to spark conversation, if the silence went on much longer I'd be off again in my analytical inner world. He wasn't going to speak up, he looked too content.

"People should be doing this every day. It's relaxing and there is the added advantage of getting to know someone without the distractions of the modern world. You can tell a lot about a person by how they react when there's no noise or commotion." He smiled at me before taking another sip of juice.

"So, you're trying to get to know me?" I popped a square of cheese into my mouth to prevent the smile that threatened to claim space on my face.

"Well, I thought it might be a good idea." He smiled revealing a double meaning behind his words. Why would it be a good idea to get to know me?

"I thought you were a loner." That's exactly how Jazz had described him. A longer, a ghost of a man who appeared just long enough to incite speculation and attention from the women before he vanished again into the night.

"Why would you think that?" He stretched his legs out and propped himself up on his elbows. His face and neck stretched toward the sun. I felt my gaze lingering on his chest; once again my breath morphed to match the push and pull of his.

"It's what everyone says," well it was what one person said. There hadn't been enough time, or desire, to take a survey from anyone else in the room.

"Oh… Jasmine," he turned his head away and grunted.

"What was that for?" I smiled because he was not the first guy to produce such a noise when referring to Jazz.

"Your friend Jasmine, she has this way of being, well really annoying," he turned to his side to face me before he popped a grape into his mouth.

"What? I don't think she is annoying," he reached for another grape, but I snatched it and popped it in my mouth. I had to take revenge for my friend somehow, besides it made him laugh. He did have a wonderful laugh.

"She has control issues. I think that's why she isn't particularly fond of me. I don't allow her to control anything. I'm sure she is feeling very proud of her little stunt in the mall right about now. But I'll let her think she was in control of the situation just this once," he smirked and grabbed another grape. I tried to snatch it again, but he saw it coming and was much quicker than I was. He held the grape between his teeth, smiling around it before biting down.

"You were in control? You planned this all out, to be alone with me?" His wanting this time with me, having already planned to take me away to what he referred to as his own little paradise, filled me with a satisfied feeling, one I hadn't felt in a long time.

It was nice to feel wanted, to know that someone in the world (outside of my bouncy best friend) cared about and looked forward to being able to spend time with me. The fact that he would go so far as to make sure that he could, well that was the cherry on top. It was nothing like the feeling I had when Jazz pestered me about returning to the land of the living. This was much better, paired with the magnetic attraction that existed between us, it anchored itself in my core.

I wasn't the only one affected by that pull, that tug that developed, pulling from my center whenever I was close to him. It was there for him just as it had been for me. The only thing I couldn't figure out was which one of us controlled it. I doubted that it was me. I'm sure I would have noticed at some point in my life if I had some invisible lasso I could wrap around a hot guy and use it to draw him to me. This was a skill that would have been used, often.

"I had to see you again." His eyes still drifted off but something in them changed. It lasted only for a second before he could regain control. Something in that moment, that eagerness mixed with a bit of concern made my blood rush.

"You just wanted to see me?" I questioned him. His sentiment was nice, quite perfect actually, it was kind of too good to believe.

"Well, obviously, more than just see," he gestured, waving his hand around him at the surroundings. "I can see you wherever you are, Alexa. I wanted to be with you, alone."

"I find it hard to believe I had that much of an effect on you. The first time you saw me, I looked a mess and felt a thousand times worse," my high faded as I remembered that first encounter. Maybe, his reasoning for this wasn't the same as mine. Perhaps this little outing was one planned out of pity for the sickly girl. Maybe he had the charitable bone, like my mother.

"I didn't see that," he lied to be nice, but there was no way he hadn't noticed.

"You already admitted that I look different today." I regretted inviting the topic into the conversation again. I still was unsure of how he felt about the details of my sudden recovery. I wrapped my arms around myself feeling self-conscious.

"Yes, you do look healthier, but that is not what drew me to you. It wasn't your looks, Alexa." He sat up and grabbed the extra blanket that was folded in the bottom of the basket, and wrapped it around me. He must have mistaken my embarrassment for a symptom of the cool air.

"Really?" Accepting the things, he said shouldn't have been that difficult, but paranoia made me think he had to have an ulterior motive. "What was it that drew you to me?"

"I can only say it was you. Not your appearance. As soon as I entered that party, before I ever saw you. I knew you were there. I could feel your presence. I lost control of myself, I wanted to go to you so badly, but I could not. It was like there was a wall there preventing me from getting closer to you. Even my words seemed to be trapped in my throat. It was the most pleasant form of terror. I found you, but I couldn't get to you." He stopped talking and searched my face, wanting a response, something that told him that he hadn't said too much. I knew that expression; it was one I often wore myself.

"That's how I felt too," My words came out low and breathy. I was afraid for him to hear, afraid the insanity of it all wasn't my own. "It was like I wasn't really me anymore. I liked the feeling; to be feeling anything at all besides pain was wonderful, but I hated it at the same time. Because, I was no longer in control of myself, and I have already lost control of so much in my life."

He leaned in closer to me again. I wanted him to kiss me, I could feel those electrical pulses initiating again throughout my body, but forced my mind to remain focused on the man that held me captive with just one look. "I know this is bizarre and I wish I could tell you what was happening, but I can't, no more than I can explain why that block, the wall that kept me from getting to you before, is not here now." He lifted his hand to my face and touched my lips with his fingertips.

"I know that I want to be with you, and that for me, is all I need to know. Life has a way of creating these inexplicable situations. I've learned that it's best not to question them, but to accept them for the marvels that they are."

Thirteen

When I opened my eyes, I was in the passenger seat of his car. My house sat outside of the window greeting me with its harsh visual welcome. He suggested that we leave shortly after I started to nod off though, it was enjoyable sitting on the blanket and soaking up the sun. He must have asked me for my address while we drove, but I didn't remember giving it to him. It didn't seem worth asking how he knew. Call me crazy; but it was oddly comforting that he did.

"I didn't want to wake you." He sat in the driver's seat next to me playing with his phone.

"How long was I asleep?" I stretched my arms and tried to hide it when it wiped my face to check for drool.

"Not long," he held back his laughter; I wasn't as subtle as I tried to be.

"I don't remember getting in the car." I yawned again and hoped my breath did not stink.

"You were out of it. I kept saying we should leave, but you wanted to stay. Eventually, I looked over and you were snoring, so I carried you to the car. I hope you don't mind. You looked so peaceful," he reached over and pulled a strand of hair out of my face tucking it behind my ear.

"You carried me?" My cheeks began to heat up. "How long have we been sitting here?"

"Not that long, only a few minutes." He smiled.

"I feel bad. I make for horrible company." First, I continued to zone out on him, and then I was snoring and drooling on his car seat. If he ever thought I was attractive, that was a thing of the past.

"Why do you say that?"

"I'm sure you didn't plan on spending the day with someone who could pass for a coma patient." I peered at him through my lashes and saw that he was still smiling at me.

"Either way, I enjoyed myself," that was all it took to make my nerves return.

"I did too…oddly." I yawned, stretched my limbs, and slumped back into the seat.

"Why oddly?"

"We barely spoke to each other; sat in silence for hours. I can only imagine how boring it must have been for you, especially after I fell asleep." Another wave of heat flooded my cheeks. They would surely be lit up now, bright enough to see from space.

"Trust me, I wasn't bored. Especially after you fell to sleep, that was the best part." His smile wavered for a moment, he was apprehensive about us and I wanted to know why, but asking would only embarrass us both. What if his answer was something obvious, something I should have already known?

"I should probably get inside. I don't want to take up too much more of your time," the decision to flee was not for his benefit. It wouldn't be long before I said or did something to scare him away.

"You don't have to go," the strain behind his words was nearly too intense for the moment. His desire to keep me near, caused me to hesitate in my escape.

If I was honest with myself, I wanted him to ask me to stay and he did. He hadn't exactly asked, but the sentiment was the same. I waited for a sign, something to tell me that I should remain in the car with him. Moments later, that sign was given to me in a spectacular way.

The gray escaped from around him not just his eyes, but all the around him, and it spread out to me. It blanketed us and erased everything else. The cool touch of it (one I must have imagined) only lasted for a second as it wrapped around me and pulled me over to him in the small space. The closer our bodies became, the more intense the heat got.

The pull was stronger now; my body jerked towards him and in an instant, I was on top of him looking down at his face. Our lips finally met as my legs straddled across his lap. The steering wheel pressed into my back. Something hot like fire, electric, raced across my skin. I closed my eyes to focus on the sensations that

127

were flooding my body, but it all seemed so overwhelming.

The pull was working to eliminate more than just my own self-control. Lacal's actions were hungry and passionate. He kissed me greedily, more than I expected from him, this gentleman who plans sweet picnics in paradise. His tongue explored my mouth, while hands were pulling at my clothes. Our breaths were now rough, deep, and in unison. The sound of fabric ripping tore me from the heat. I pulled back to look at him, the jolt I felt was echoed back to me in his expression. I felt the pieces of fabric before I saw them.

In my hands were shreds of his white shirt, I stared at them, and then to his bare chest. He started to say something; whatever it was, I imagined wasn't going to be good, so I grabbed my bags and darted from the car.

Running to my door, there were no sounds of him following me, no attempt to stop my retreat. I hoped he was just stunned, and not totally disgusted with me. Once in the house, I threw my keys to the floor and slammed the door behind me. Humiliation began to choke me, and my legs turned to jelly. I slid to the floor with my back pressed against the wood barrier. A few minutes passed and the panic began to subside. The sound of his engine came to me from outside, purring as he drove away.

My mind was unable to process what it had just experienced. I hadn't been able to govern my own actions. Yes, this had happened before, a symptom of my illness, but then it was spasms that wracked my limbs, not passion. This was different; I had been controlled by impulse. The pleasure of it was 100 times more penetrating than any pain I had ever felt. I pulled myself off the floor and headed for the stairs.

What did he think of me? He'd been so nice all day, only to get attacked and ran out on. He had to have experienced the same thing; I hadn't been there alone. The heat of his skin on mine felt too real to be something my mind had fabricated. What about the gray? Surely, I had imagined that sensation of it touching my skin, color didn't have the ability to touch!

I still held the pieces of his shirt in my hand. I put them to my nose, inhaling the scent, sweet, yet musky, perfect! Where the hell did the strength come from to rip through the fabric? What was found beneath the shirt, was far from disappointing. The small groan escaped my lips as the image of his bare chest returned. Even more so, the feeling of the heavy rise and fall was so much better when pressed against my own chest. His abs felt like they had been set in stone. In any other situation, I would have been able to enjoy it all. However, after the time we spent together, the heat, the fire, the sensuality of it all. The connection I wanted to be real, it only worked to convince me that I was indeed dreaming.

As I reached the top of the stairs, the shower called to me much louder than my bed did. I had slept enough, and after what had just taken place, my body was excited. A shower would help to calm the urge I had to run out into the streets and track him down. After setting the temperature of the water, I decided to check my reflection. It may have been vain, but it was hard not to be excited about seeing the girl who looked back, this new and improved me.

Reflected back to me was more than just the new face, full of health and life. It was also the evidence of what had just taken place, evidence that the passion in the car was not just my own. If what I had done to his shirt was bad, this could only be classified as criminal. My top was completely shredded! In my race to get away from him, I never thought to check the damage done to my own attire. My bra was exposed beneath my torn top and one strap was missing entirely. My hair was no longer in the ponytail, but stood wildly over my head like a mad woman. With my luck, one of my neighbors had seen me running to the safety of my home. There were so many ways for that scene to be misinterpreted. The police would be out searching for his car within minutes! If I had thought to get his phone number, I would have called to warn him. On the other hand, I may have told him to come back. So, what if he would be risking jail time!

My jeans were unbuttoned, and the zipper was gone. Great, they were my favorite pair. That was when I noticed the hickies, little blood clots that had formed under my skin where he had kissed me, created by the pull of his lips. There were two on my neck and one on my left breast. I couldn't even remember that happening. Damn, how could any feeling be strong enough to block out the sensation of him ravaging my body?

The red spot on my breast still throbbed with the blood that had been pulled there. I touched the skin and felt it pulsate underneath my finger, my heart drummed faster and sent my mind back again, back to the car. Only this time there was no mental interference between me and the feel of his touch, the way his fingertips danced across my skin. It all played in slow motion. There was no rigid movement that brought me to my place on top of him. My body flowed as I threw my leg across him and settled in on his lap. My fingers combed through his hair before grabbing a handful and pulling his mouth to mine.

My head fell back, a smile wide across my face, as I guided his mouth to my neck. Then lower, his tongue traced the curves of my throat as his mouth found my breast. I could feel my skin giving way to him. Inviting him in as my chest rose to the heat of his breath, encouraging him to continue.

My breath became more shallow and chaotic as his hands tore apart my shirt and pulled my bra strap down with so much force it snapped off completely, and landed in the passenger seat. I pulled the rubber band out of my hair as his hands found the button of my jeans. He tugged it once and the zipper went flying to the back seat.

He looked at me, desire filling his eyes, like the flame that created that smoky gray that surrounded us. He was trying to control himself and catch his breath. He didn't get a chance, I dove into him again teasing his lip between my teeth until he lost control as his hands travelled across my body gripping and releasing as he tried to regain some composure. His left hand pulled my hair, while the right slipped under my shirt and cupped my breast.

Greedily, I invited him into myself and took all that I could. My fingers wrapped around his collar and pulled, instead of the ripping sound I heard before, the doorbell rang out from downstairs.

I shut off the shower and walked down the stairs pulling a new shirt over my head, and trying to stop my heart from beating through my chest. This reaction was one of anticipation, not the nervous response that had happened repeatedly throughout the day. Standing at the bottom of the staircase, I realized who this anticipation was for. I wanted Lacal; I hoped it was him on the other side of the door. I hoped he had come back to finish what we had started.

My pulse picked up again and my head swam as I felt the heat of his lap return to the space between my legs. A few deep breaths to center myself proved pointless. The pull he had over me wasn't there, but I

132

was going to the door anyway. My body, or something deep inside of me, couldn't wait to be with him again.

I paused again before turning the doorknob and considered running back up the stairs to my bed to wait for this to be over. This dream was too much, too real, too dangerous to continue to play into. I was getting in too deep, which is exactly what I said I wouldn't do.

The fantasy had gotten to me, it convinced me to get lost in the glamour of it all, and now I was anticipating more. The best course of action would be to let go of the illusion, because becoming more involved would result in my destruction when I finally woke up, and I knew that it would happen eventually. The feelings in the car, and everything that took place since our first encounter, none of it could possibly be real. The pain had to have caught up with me at Jazz's party. I must be lying on her floor passed out, and probably never even made it to my car. Perhaps I was in an ambulance or in a coma, locked away in my own mind.

Ready to accept this and retreat to my room, I turned away, but the bell rang again. My heart jumped, strayed from its predetermined rhythm. Lacal. His name skittered through my mind. I wanted him and if he was there, he wouldn't be refused. One more cleansing breath and I opened the door.

Fourteen

"I want to know everything!" Jazz burst through the door before I could even fully turn the knob. She walked past me into the living room, and threw herself across the couch with her feet slung over the armrest. Her arms were crossed under her head, and her lips poked out like an impatient child.

I took my time closing the door and walking into the room, deliberately dragging my feet along the floor. I needed to get my thoughts in order and deal with this new mixture of feelings. The relief to see my friend, yet annoyance that I couldn't continue my fantasy, and satisfy that part inside of me that longed to be with Lacal.

What approach should I use in dealing with my eager friend? She'd come for one thing only and that was information, but how much should she be told? She would have her own opinions about what happened. Most likely, they would make me feel naïve and point out my overreaction to everything. That reality check wasn't necessary.

REVITALIZED

Joining the emotional cocktail was my good old friend, Embarrassment. I could only imagine what Jazz would think, but what about Lacal? Maybe that was the reason he had left without looking back. Hell, he was probably already with his friends, laughing and joking about it. Telling them about the girl who ripped his shirt off and ran away.

Across the room from my eager friend, I dropped down onto the loveseat, and ignored the huffs and puffs she directed at me. It wasn't possible to continue my avoidance any longer, Jazz wouldn't allow it. She was only giving me time to adjust, to get my thoughts in order, very generous coming from her. Jazz was an impatient one, a side of her I was well acquainted with.

She sat up, threw her arms in the air, and groaned. "So, how long is this going to take?"

"What?" anything, including playing dumb for was worth a shot if it would hold off the conversation she had come to have.

"Look, I know you've been out of the real world for a while, but damn!" She sat up on the couch and faced me with stern eyes. "Dish…now!"

"What is it that you want to know?" I fluttered my eyelashes innocently playing with fire.

"Everything," she rolled her eyes and sucked her teeth.

"More specific please," buying more time, I smiled.

"Okay, so now I have to put on my detective hat and dig for the dirt?" She crossed her legs shaking her foot in the air. "Where did y'all go?"

"Go?" I tried to look perplexed, but only managed a sad level of childish mocking.

"Well, I know for a fact that you didn't come straight home." She smiled slyly making no effort to hide her pride about her insight.

"How?"

She cocked her head to the side and winked. Jazz had eyes and ears all over Chicago, and finding out whether I came home or not wouldn't exactly be a challenge for her.

"Stop stalling and tell me what happened."

"Nothing happened," I lied. "Well, at least nothing that you would consider interesting."

She let out an exhausted sigh and rolled her eyes.

"We went to this little park, I don't know where, we talked, and then sat there for hours not talking. I fell asleep on the blanket, and when I woke up I was home," I spat out the facts as fast as I could, trailing off and purposely excluding the events that unfolded after I woke up in his car.

"Blanket," she said suspiciously, already detecting the holes in my story. I swear the girl really could be a top private eye. "Where, when, and how does a blanket come into play?"

"He set up this little picnic for us," she was asking too many questions already, soon she would get it out of me. I leaned back on the loveseat and hoped my defenses were stronger now.

"Oh, so there was a picnic?" She raised her eyebrows expecting the news to get even juicier.

"Yeah, one of those fruit and veggie platters and some juice, nothing special," I was trying to dismiss the subject, but my gut told me that she was not about to let it go.

"Oh, so you just had a picnic, sat and talked…" she searched for a weak point to dig her nails in deeper. "And what did we learn about Lacal?" Eyes lit up, she leaned forward on the couch, anxious to finally know more about the only person to ever elude her.

"Not much, I did most of the talking," disappointment spread across her face, giving me some hope that this would be enough to kill the topic.

"Great, the one time you should be reserved, you can't stop talking? Now I have to pull teeth to get scraps of information," She let out another exasperated sigh and got off the couch. "So, you got anything to eat?"

I was relieved to be off the subject even though there was no chance it would last long. Eventually Jazz would come up with more questions for me to answer. I followed her into the kitchen feeling relieved that she hadn't decided to leave. That would have left me alone with my thoughts again, and I knew all too well how those could take a path of their own, leading me in any number of directions. Most of which, I had no intentions of going. Not while Jazz, private eye, was on the scene.

Leaning on the counter, I watched as Jazz raided the kitchen finding all the ingredients she needed. She made a sandwich that looked too big for her to consume. However, I had no doubt that she could. She cut up some melon, and grabbed a bottle of orange juice from the fridge; all before snagging a bag of chips out of the pantry. I was sure they had to be stale, but for Jazz that would mean nothing but a change in flavor.

Her appetite hadn't changed. If it wasn't for the two hours she worked out every morning, she wouldn't be able to fit through the door. It was a love-hate relationship that she had with food. She loved to eat it, but she hated the aftermath, or should I say what she had to do to prevent the aftermath.

She sat at the table and began to dig in. I followed her lead, grabbed a few strawberries, and sat across the table from her. It didn't escape me how easy sitting there had become. Yes, the fact that I noticed at all most likely meant that I still had a few lingering qualms, but they weren't enough to make me want to move away. I summed it up to being around Jazz, and the comfort of old times she brought with her.

Fifteen

"Not hungry?" She asked, eyeing the handful of fruit I had as she smashed her sandwich to a height that would fit into her mouth.

"Not really."

"You got a lot on your mind?" That hungry look was in her eyes, the kind that could only be satisfied with gossip, not food.

"I don't know," nothing except the lack of distraction Jazz had actually been able to provide me with.

"Is it Lac-aaaal?" She started to resume the inquisition. She stretched out the sound of his name, teasing me.

"I guess," downplaying the situation was my only disguise and it was a weak one.

"What about him?" She crunched into a stale chip and smiled at me.

"He is just so…intense," I popped a piece of the fruit in my mouth and attempted once again to organize my thoughts.

"What do you mean by that?" She cocked her head to the side.

"I'm not sure. It's something about him that draws me in and I start to feel like I am losing myself" Already, I was giving her way to much information, but talking about it was actually making it easier to sort out.

"Sounds hot," she slurped her juice and stared at me, eager for more dirt.

"In a way it is, but it's also kind of scary. I don't exactly enjoy not being able to control myself." I had lost interest in eating the fruit and played with it in my hands.

"Especially, if it's one sided," her claws dug further forcing me to give in. She knew that would make me want to defend myself. What girl wants to look as if she is pining after someone who in return, isn't interested?

"I don't think it is," I tossed it out there and waited for her response. My stomach began to knot up.

"For real?" This was all she managed to choke out. I thought she would tell me it was impossible and confirm my fears that I had managed to imagine an attraction that was not there.

"Yeah, but I could be wrong. You know I haven't had to do much analyzing of the opposite sex for a while, but I am pretty sure he was just as into me as I was him." Remembering his face as he fought to hold back while I was in his lap, it had to be true, especially considering the condition of my torn jeans! Damn, I would never find another pair that fit like that.

"Girl one day out of your coma and you already got Mr. Untouchable, head over heels for you? You do realize that a lot of girls are going to want to kill you now, right? I mean damn, they will be out for blood!" She laughed and was now leaning across the table, eyes bucked, and waiting for more.

Looking across the table at my eager friend, I wanted to tell Jazz everything. I had been out of the 'real world' for a long time and it couldn't hurt to get some outside perspective on this situation. Especially, from someone like Jazz who held the title of expert in all things social.

"Something else happened," I dropped the teaser, knowing she would bite.

"Really? What?" Yeah, she was hooked.

"Well, I kind of attacked him," my body froze, bracing for impact.

"Attacked?" She dropped the piece of fruit she was about to pop into her already stuffed mouth, and scooted to the edge of her seat. Her hands slammed on the table frightening me. I shook it off and continued.

"One second I'm getting ready to hop out of his car, and the next, I'm like straddled across his lap; kissing him, and ripping his shirt off," I put my hands over my face hoping my cheeks hadn't turned as red as they felt.

"Ripping his shirt off?! Oh my God girl," She took a swig of juice to help wash down the food in her mouth, so she wouldn't choke when she rolled her neck at me. "You sat here trying to bore me to death with blankets and picnics when you have juice like this?"

"It's just that I'm not exactly sure how he reacted. I kind of ran out of the car and into the house."

"So, you attacked him and then fled the scene of the crime?" She let out a snicker that thankfully helped ease the tension.

"Yeah, something like that," I sighed and leaned back in my seat dropping my head back to stare at the ceiling.

"Well, did he...attack back?" My moment of hesitation told her there was something more. "What?"

The abrupt pressure on my chest caused me to gasp. What the hell was that? Eagerness, that's what it was, the wave of anticipation, it came from her and physically smashed into me. I felt like my chest would cave in from the weight of her gaze alone. This was new; Lacal was the only one I had ever experienced that sensation with. The emotions, they were intense, and yet, they were not my own. The tangible force pressed against me harder. It was much stronger with Lacal, but it was the same feeling. I stared at her and for a brief moment, I saw the colors of sunset outlining her figure, made of hints of bright red and orange. It was there then I blinked, and it was gone. Perhaps I was more tired than I thought.

REVITALIZED

"My clothes didn't exactly survive the encounter either," if I hadn't continued, she would have jumped me.

"I knew something was up when I saw your change in wardrobe!" She shrieked with pleasure while simultaneously eyeing the wrinkled shirt I had thrown on with contempt.

The worst should have never been expected from Jazz. She was still the same girl I'd always known; hungry for gossip, and easily excitable. My own self-conscious had me bracing to be judged and ridiculed, but she did neither. Truthfully, I would be the same way if the tables were turned. Looking from the outside in, what happened in the car would appear more exhilarating than confusing.

"I didn't even realize it until I was upstairs," I thought of my appearance, clothes torn, hair wild and heat rushing all over my body as the details of what happened in the car replayed inside my head.

"Okay, so I have to agree, it's definitely not one sided. Now, tell me, what is the problem here?" She thought I should be pursuing this. I had my reasons for not doing so. Reasons I did not know how to explain. Like clouds of gray that left their cool touch on my skin!

"The problem is that, as you pointed out, I have barely been out of my 'coma' for a day, and all of this is overwhelming right now. I mean, for all I know, tomorrow I could be right back where I was before. Then what happens?" I got up from the table and tossed the remainder of the fruit into the trash, welcome back anxiety! The best bet was to get my body moving or panic would set in.

"You're worrying way too much, Lex. I think you should be enjoying this, enjoying him. Nothing says you have to be with him forever, and like you said, tomorrow you could be right back where you were before. Do you want to be sitting up regretting the fact that you didn't let yourself live while you had the chance?"

I looked at my friend and felt the truth in her words, echoing Lacal's sentiment. I should enjoy this marvel for all that he was. I'd become afraid to live. For so long, my life was too fragile to consider taking any type of risk. My concern was more for schedules and appointments than being alive. Over time, the world had fallen out of my reach. Here was my chance to jump back in and potentially have some real fun and I was turning my back on it.

Jazz finished swallowing down her meal, and we returned to the comfort of the living room. There we sat for hours talking nonstop first going over all the details of what happened with Lacal. Jazz took little time before dissecting all of his actions, my actions, movements and statements so that she could start spouting off her analysis of what each little thing meant under her social microscope.

By the end of it all, I felt like I was the top suspect in a murder investigation and had just finished being interrogated by the F.B.I. Her conclusion was that the attraction and chemistry was mutual, no question about it. She also felt my running from the car wouldn't be a big deal if he liked me as much as she thought he did. I would be lying if I said I'd hoped she was wrong.

From there, she began to go down the list of all the girls who were sure to absolutely hate my guts once word got out, which with Jazz wouldn't be very long. I'm sure she sent a text out to the masses when I went to get us the leftover tea from the fridge. Apparently, there was a long queue of girls who had attempted to interact with Lacal on a more than friendship basis. If he did respond, it was only to politely turn down the offer of their company. Learning this was a major stroke to the ego. After listening to her catalog, the names of the girls, (some of whom could be considered the top of the womanly food chain, the hardest to get) not being able to grab his attention, my confidence was shooting sky high.

Unfortunately, that feeling didn't last long before it twisted inside me and transformed itself. All of Jazz's encouragement began to burn, and quickly turned to ash by my own insecurity. I couldn't compete with those girls and yet, he had turned them all down. How long would it take for him to realize that?

What was it that he could have possibly seen in me that was so special? What did he expect from me? Would I be able to keep him interested? I wasn't even sure what it was I had done to spark his interest to begin with! With that, the remainder of my newfound confidence fizzled away.

Jazz left a little after four in the morning. We finished the night off scanning through channels, and making fun of random reality shows. After locking up the house, I hauled myself up the stairs to my bed. As I climbed underneath my covers, I could only think that this fatigue settling over me meant that I was close to waking up from the dream that I still refused to accept as reality. I closed my eyes and waited.

Sixteen

Staring up from my pillow, the intricate web of cracks in my ceiling that usually welcomed me awake was missing. Instead, there was a gray sky filled with storm clouds that looked as if they were moments from opening up and drowning me. Low rumbles of thunder shook the bed violently. I placed my back against the headboard reaching out to hold the edge to avoid being tossed off. I found my hold just seconds before my chest was crushed by the strongest blast of wind I had ever felt. It pushed all the air out of my lungs, causing my body to jerk. Tears ran down my face as I wished for the pain to be over and suddenly it was.

My body collapsed to the bed and I attempted to breathe. Oxygen burned as it spilled into my lungs. I lay there gasping for air and trying to calm the trembling of my body. Finally, I managed to still my nerves and pulled myself up from the mattress to scan the space around me. Afraid to move, my heart sunk into my stomach when I found nothing I could use to save me. I was trapped in emptiness, a void with no end in sight. Beneath the bed, there didn't look to be anything solid for me to step out onto.

Another current of air came, but it streamed from underneath me. This time lifting the bed and tilting it to one side. I scrambled to hold on and reached for the opposite side. Now I was flying into the air and barely grasped the edge of the bed frame to avoid falling into the abyss.

The bed slammed down and made a sound like thunder, it caused my body to flail into the air, but my hands still held on tightly to the bed. My stomach slammed on the edge of the bed frame and almost caused me to lose my grip. I lay there not wanting to move again. Trembling all over, I needed to figure a way out, but I couldn't hear my thoughts over the sound of my pulse beating in my ear.

Above the rhythm of my heart, I could just barely make out what sounded like screaming. My pulse raced, and the blood continued roaring in my ears, mixing with the shrill sound that began to grow in volume. It was seconds before I realized that the scream was coming from my own lips. My head pivoted faster, scanning the space around me, hoping for something, anything that could appear as a savior for me.

Panic gripped me, and my muscles seized. It wasn't because of the wind that had picked up. It blew even harder than the infamous Hawk that often ravished the streets of Chicago, I could stand those winds, I was used to that, this wind was different. It scared the hell out of me because some part of me, that same evasive, unknown part that called out for Lacal and clawed at me whenever I was near my grandmother, knew that there was something to fear.

REVITALIZED

Only now, instead of trying to take over and force my actions against my will, it was warning me that something was coming for me and yelling at me to find a way out. It gave me the energy I needed to bring life back to my body. As I pulled myself up again, I felt something move behind me. I turned, inhaled quickly, and held my breath afraid to make a sound.

This wasn't just emptiness surrounding me, just a layer of darkness. Looking closer, I could see that it was moving. It was tangible, and if I reached out I could touch it, I felt the chill that came from it, this dark thing. If it got the chance, it would destroy me.

It moved with a contemptuous display of life, the wind blew again only this time it registered feeling more like a breath; the powerful cold, and stale breath of this thing. It started to engulf the bed, attempting to swallow it whole and take me with it. It crept towards me devouring the mattress, I watched as it disappeared into nothingness. I smashed my back against what was left of the headboard and tried to pull myself as far away from it as I could get. Hopelessness wrapped around me like a paralyzing blanket; there was nothing left to do and nowhere to go.

Reluctantly I gave in to the inevitability of it. All I could do was try to focus on anything but the pain I was sure to endure once it reached me. I closed my eyes tightly and waited for the onslaught. Pain was nothing new to my body; years spent living in agony had to be worse than anything this thing could do to me, I could only hope it would be over quickly. Instead of pain, I felt my body moving, hovering, I wanted to know what was happening, but I couldn't bring myself to open my eyes.

Warmth healed the spots on my skin where its icy breath left me frostbitten. The feeling of hovering stopped, and my body was lowered onto a hard, flat surface. I kept my eyes closed and ignored the false relief. Clearly, this thing wanted my attention when it attacked. As soon as I relaxed or dropped my guard, pain would follow just as it had before. Maybe, if I could ignore it long enough, it would go away. It was a long shot, but it was worth a try.

There was a sound, familiar yet strange; it didn't belong here in this empty hell. I tried to block it out. Surely, it was another trick, anything to get me to open my eyes, and bear witness to my own slaughter. I repeatedly told myself that it was a joke and not to open my eyes. The warmth intensified on my shoulders and then I felt that pull again, the one that matched the sound. It reached out to me, not to swallow me but to give me the reassurance of my safety. The sound was there again, this time the bond we had, forced me to open my mind and listen.

"Alexa, please wake up," his voice was soothing yet urgent. "Open your eyes. We have to go!"

I did as he asked and opened my eyes. I was lying on the ground staring up at him and when I saw him, I removed the lock I had put on myself and let my senses bring me back to life. The warm breeze carried the scent of flowers replacing the stale stench that originated from whatever that thing was. The darkness was gone. Behind his head, I could see the sun. When I was able to see his face to know for sure that it wasn't some terrible trick, I smiled at him and relaxed instantly.

He grabbed my hand and lifted me from the ground. His arms wrapped around me and embraced me tightly. His scent mingled with the flowers and created an aroma that made my heart race. I was happy to be there with him and never wanted to leave. It would have been perfect if he never let me go, but he did.

"We have to go." This was all he said before he turned, making sure he had hold of my hand, and started to run. I followed him; no questions asked. We ran. I waited for my body to give out, but it never did. I held his hand tightly and continued to run.

My eyes opened again this time revealing my room. The cracks staring back at me provided me with confidence; I was safe now and I could feel it. My body lay there waiting for the dark void to return to take me, but it wouldn't. I was safe, the nightmare was over which meant I was back in my old body, back to my old life. The dream had ended, and it was a nightmare, just as I thought it would be.

It was still dark outside. I hadn't slept that long. I waited. I knew the pain would return now that the dream had concluded. In fact, I was sure of it. I watched the digits flicker on the clock, time passing, one hour, two, the sun rose and still I felt nothing. I couldn't keep lying to myself. This was no dream, no illusion; Nana's cure had worked!

Seventeen

I stretched my body, and smiled at the ease. No aftershocks, no more pain. I whispered a thank you to my grandmother and an apology to my mother. I was whole again. How could I not be happy? How could I not smile? It was all real, he was real!

I stood in the shower and let it rejuvenate my body. A shower had never felt so good. It was almost as if I was absorbing energy from the water as I thought of the blue liquid that healed my body. I stayed under the stream until the hot water was gone and the chill set in.

No cold shock was needed to shoot through my legs to wake me up, no solemn walk down the stairs looking at faces long lost to me. It was nice to stray from my usual morning routine. I could bypass the pills that waited to puncture my throat. Instead, I walked to the fridge and took out twice the amount of my normal helping of fruit. I finished it and my stomach growled wanting more. My appetite had increased as well. I guess healthy people were the ones who ate.

The house phone rang twice before I picked it up off the counter, juggling the bowl and a bottle of water in my free hand. I answered through a mouthful of fruit, and like déjà vu, I nearly choked when I heard the voice on the other end.

"Alexa?"

"Yeah," I couldn't think of anything else to say.

"I just wanted to make sure you were okay." Lacal spoke to me, his voice low, as if he had just woken up.

"I…um…I'm fine. Why?" I took a quick swig of water while I waited for his response.

"After what happened yesterday I was worried that perhaps I did something wrong, something to offend you. I planned to stay away but last night I had a disturbing dream about you. I had to make sure you were okay." He cleared his throat trying to erase the traces of sleep from his voice.

"A dream?" It had to be a coincidence, of course we were dreaming about each other after our encounter.

"Yes." He sounded off, distracted.

"About?" Something told me I did not want to know but I asked the question anyway.

"Nothing really, it was weird, mildly upsetting," he paused; his attempt to downplay his feelings was even more transparent than mine. "When I awoke, I had this nagging urge to make sure that you were not harmed."

"Oh," I decided not to tell him about my dream. I could have, and he would have believed it. He would have seen the similarities, the connection. I knew he

154

would, but I was not sure if I believed it myself. I found myself questioning if there was some deeper connection between us, more than physical attraction, but stuff like psychic links and coinciding dreams, didn't happen in real life.

"Would it be possible for me to see you today?" His question caught me off guard.

"Today?" Okay, I had to stop questioning everything he said. He might take it the wrong way; think that I was searching for an excuse not to see him.

"Yes. That is, only if you are not busy with something else. I'd like to be able to see you again." there it was, he thought I was searching for an excuse not to see him.

His invitation was unexpected. After how I acted the night before, I was sure that he would disappear. After all, that is what he was known for, his vanishing act. However, he hadn't vanished, he was right there on the other end of the phone, dreaming about me, and asking to see me again.

"Yes, that would be okay. There is nothing on my agenda that I'm aware of," I tried not to sound too eager. Nevertheless, there was no way that I could say no. Besides, I wanted to know more about his dream. I would need to find a way to ease it into the conversation.

"Oh…good," shocked by my response, he quickly continued. "What time should I pick you up?"

I looked at the clock, it was already 11:30, "Give me a couple of hours. I should be decent enough by then," my attempt at a joke failed.

"Okay, I will give you a call when I'm close to you." I could hear his smile, the way it wrapped around his words and couldn't wait to see it in person again.

"Great." Could he hear my smile in the same way?

Ending the call, his words echoed in my head, the idea of him coming to me, being close to me again, had my expectations rising. I had to do a better job of keeping my actions in check this time around. No more ripped shirts or destroyed jeans. I stood by the counter and chose not to question how he got my number. He never asked me for it, but of all the things that had happened in the last few days, this had to be the least suspicious. There were any number of ways for him to acquire a phone number and I was sure I knew the one that had worked for him.

I picked up the phone; there was only one person who could help me now, that person was most likely waiting for my call. I was looking for some reassurance and Jazz would be the perfect person for the job, unless it backfired and caused my countless number of insecurities to continue to grow. To be honest, it could go either way.

"Hello?" She picked up after the first ring.

"Hey Jazz." I sighed.

"What's up Lex?" She sounded breathless, no doubt just finishing up her morning workout.

"He called," no messing around, his name was unnecessary. There was only one person I could be talking about. Ignoring how pathetic that sounded.

"Really? What did he say?" She struggled for a moment to catch her breath.

"He asked if he could see me today. Are you okay? You sound like you're going to pass out."

"Yeah, working out, you know I have to battle the arrival of my mother's hips," she laughed. "So, what did you say?"

"I said yes." I didn't have the heart to tell her that her mom's hips had already found her, I am sure she was aware.

"Good, I was afraid you would flake out, I almost called to give you the heads up."

"You knew he was going to call!?" I tried to fake the sound of shock, but of course I wasn't surprised. There was no way Jazz would pass up on getting an in with him. She probably made him trade his own digits for the information.

"Yeah, he called and asked me for your number this morning. To be honest, I was surprised you hadn't given it to him yesterday. But there probably wasn't any time for that, what with you molesting him and running away," she laughed, and I could hear her gulping down what I assumed was either Gatorade or water.

"Well, I didn't flake out. Of course, I'm not sure if I want to do this. He said he will be here in a couple hours to pick me up."

"Why would you not be sure Alexa?" she sounded both amused and frustrated.

"You can't be serious, clearly *you* haven't forgotten about what took place yesterday, and you weren't even there. How am I supposed to face him?" I thought about the shredded fabric that was still on my bathroom floor.

"No, I haven't," another snicker. "But, I'm telling you it was not a big deal to him. Maybe you shouldn't be making it one for you."

"Too late for that, and thanks for your support. I'm glad I can provide you with such comic relief," I rolled my eyes and huffed.

"Oh, don't be like that. Look, you seriously need to chill out. You said he will be there in a couple hours. Take that time to get yourself together. You know, try to relax. Pamper yourself a little. And please, please find something decent to wear." She laughed, I smiled.

"Okay, now I feel insulted," I didn't, how could she expect me to care about my wardrobe when my first two days back to life had already been so full of drama? If I had on clothes, well that was a job well done as far as I was concerned.

"Well you should. Now, use that feeling to motivate you to fix the problem. I'm being serious now girl, it's like all the years of fashion sense I gave you crawled up in a hole somewhere and died." She gagged.

"Ouch," I took a deep breath already regretting the question before it had made it pass my lips. "What do you suggest I wear?"

Jazz had my entire wardrobe catalogued in her head. It took her no time to give me a piece-by-piece map of what I should choose. She matched one of the new shirts she made me buy with some black Capri jeans she said gave my butt the right amount of perkiness. She also chose my shoes, a low wedge heeled sandal, subtle jewelry, and she also told me how to do my hair. All of which, I promised I would follow exactly as she instructed.

I took her directions, happy that I wouldn't have to mull over the choices myself. It made getting ready a lot simpler. I would have to consider doing this daily. I approached it as a checklist, but forgot to take my time. Finishing up, I looked pretty good, but there was almost a full hour left on the clock.

Not wanting to risk having to endure another round of critiques from Jazz about my failing fashion sense, I decided to pass the time by doing my nails. I could remember the days when I would spend hours working on my hands. Filing, buffing and polishing as carefully as I could, it was a form of meditation. By the end, I would feel relaxed and centered, and have cute nails to show for it. The effect was the same as I prepped my paws and thought of him, I felt very Zen like.

As he said he would, Lacal called to give me a heads up that he was getting close to my house. I thanked him for the advanced warning. This would give me time to get all my things together and eliminate the chance of forgetting something important as I ran to the door. I heard his car pull up in front of the house. As agreed on the phone, I got ready to go out to the car, but as I reached the door, there was an unexpected knock. I opened it to find Lacal standing there.

"Oh... did you need something?" I took a step back.

"Um, no," he looked nervous, almost guarded as he scanned the room behind me. "Are you okay?"

"Yeah, I'm fine. Why?" I turned and followed his eyes with my own. I had taken me a bit longer than expected to grab my things, but that gave no reason for him to be concerned. Hell, I am a girl, of course I had to triple check everything!

"So, you're ready to go?" All trace of caution was gone. I smiled because it was a complete comfort to know that I wasn't the only weird one in this relationship.

Relationship? This couldn't actually be called a relationship at this point could it? It was still too soon to be searching for any definition of what was going on between us. I wouldn't be the one to pump it up to being more than what it was. Like the desperate people who would change their relationship status on Facebook too soon, going from 'single' to 'in a relationship', only to be embarrassed when the other person never makes the switch.

"Yes, I'm ready. So where are we going today? You never mentioned, and I never asked." I smiled again as I closed the door behind me.

Eighteen

"If it's okay with you, I thought we could go to my place." At this point, we were walking back to his car and his back was to me, but it sounded like he was nervous that I would decide that I didn't want to go.

"You want to take me to your place?" I stopped by the car, this time waiting for him to open the door which made him smile.

"Yeah, it's only fair. I know so much about you. Now it's your turn to learn a bit about me." He winked at me.

"You know so much about me? How?" We stood with the door between us, it was a good thing too because the smell of him was causing my brain to formulate irrational thoughts.

"Apart from the nonstop gossiping since your 'rise from the dead', as most people seem to be referring to it, you were pretty talkative yesterday," another smile paired with a quick wink.

"Oh," there wasn't really any other way to respond. Jazz had been right about the gossip circulating about me. I had been off the grid for a while, but that wasn't what mattered here. The gossiping wasn't really about me. It was about Lacal and his unlikely attraction to me.

"Don't be embarrassed." He smiled, this time a bit softer, more careful.

"I'm not. I guess I hadn't realized that I was such a hot topic. Though, I shouldn't be all that surprised considering the recent events."

"I would say you should be more flattered than anything," he leaned over the door lowering his face to mine. I inhaled him, and my head felt light.

"Flattered? Why would I be flattered by gossip?" My voice threatened to give out, but I kept myself steady.

"It's not only gossip, there happens to be a lot of jealousy in there as well." He took a deep breath, inhaling my own scent and smiling.

"Jealousy? Who would possibly be jealous of me?" Besides the hordes of girls that were pining for Lacal, I couldn't think of anything that would possibly inspire any level of envy.

"You would be surprised."

He motioned for me to get in. I did, this time with more confidence. Though it took a bit of concentration not to be overwhelmed by the memory of what took place the last time I was in his car. He got in and started to drive without looking at me. I wasn't the only one who felt embarrassed. I tried to run through the reasons why I shouldn't go, all the warnings they dish out to us good girls about the bad boys of the world. None of them seemed enough to do the trick, to convince me to dispute his choice of destination. I smiled as I hopped in the car and giggled when I heard his sigh of relief.

"So how long have you lived in Chicago?" The car cruised down the street away from my house.

"About a year, though technically I don't live in Chicago."

"Technically, where do you live?"

"Wheeling."

"Oh. Far." I knew the place well; when I was younger, I would often go for drives out to that area with my father for his job. I loved the days he would let me tag along and meet his clients, though I had no idea what he did. Whenever I would ask, he would give me a long, complicated, answer filled with big words that explained nothing. Like many other things, I eventually stopped questioning it.

"If it's too far, I could turn back," he slowed the car, so he would be able to turn around if I wanted him to, I didn't.

"No, no, it's not too far, just unexpected. You know, word is you're around Chicago a lot," I remembered Jazz's statement about him showing up and searching most of her parties. I wondered if he had been searching for me, but quickly tossed the thought aside. "It just seems a long way to go, especially, when you don't know too many people."

164

"What makes you think I don't know many people here?" He smiled as he stepped on the gas.

"Well as far as Jazz's hounds have reported, you are a loner. You pop in and out of places without so much as a 'hi' to anyone."

"That would make me look like a loner, I suppose."

"Do you mean to say that you're not?" I tilted my face to get a better view of his; it looked like I was making him uncomfortable.

"Not exactly..." he trailed off.

"And that means?" I nudged him to continue.

"Here in Chicago I am, I suppose, but at home, where I'm from it's quite the opposite." His smile was one of longing; he wanted to be home again.

"And where is that?"

"Far away," he deliberately avoided looking at me, to hide the sadness that I heard in his tone.

"Okay…" something told me it would be best not to press the issue here, at least not yet. I hoped that there would be a better time to bring it back up.

I stared out the window not sure how to continue the conversation. There was so much left to find out about him. I was afraid to move forward. It wasn't really a product of fear, more like listening to my instincts. Before, I would have ignored it, that thing that sounds the alarms and warns me to retreat. This time I would listen to it and back off. Eventually, the reason for that urge to pull back would come to light, so I put little effort towards trying to figure it out.

His house was nothing special; actually, it was pretty plain, although very large. It blended in with all the other beige and brown colored homes that neighbored it; very suburban. He turned the car into the driveway and stopped inside the garage. The door closed before the engine stopped running. I waited for him to move before getting out of the car.

The garage that was connected to the side of his house seemed fitting for him. Closed off from the world, it was as Jazz had described him. I wondered if his neighbors ever saw his face. With his tinted windows and remaining inside of his car until the garage door closed; if I were his neighbor, I would have been suspicious. Concocting theories of bodies buried in the basement. Maybe they saw him as that creepy guy on the block, the one no one would ever approach.

Come to think of it, it was possible that my own neighbors may have similar theories about me. I lived pretty much the same way, hidden away from the world, never being seen. We were the same, well if you take away the cookie cutter house.

The décor inside was annoyingly ordinary. I wanted to see something that screamed Lacal, but there were only the necessities and not much furniture at all. It appeared that he lived alone; which had me wondering about his family. Where were they and why wasn't he with them? I supposed that was the reason for the sad tone in his voice when he referred to home being 'far away'.

My heart ached as I cataloged the similarities between our lives. We were both alone, and longing for families that we could no longer be with. I followed him through the house and into the kitchen. Everything was modern and once again simple, only what was essential. There were black granite counters, with tile in neutral tones, beiges and browns, surrounding all the stainless-steel appliances.

He took two bottles of water from the refrigerator, handed me one and nodded for me to take a seat at the counter. He didn't say anything, just stared at me, the longer the silence lasted, the more uncomfortable I became.

"You look nervous...why?" He tossed the bottle in the air with his left and caught it with his right.

"Honestly?" I played with my bottle in my hands.

"Preferably," he took the cap off the bottle and started guzzling it apparently, he was thirstier than I was. He tossed the empty bottle in the trash and went for another one.

"This isn't what I had in mind for the day, that's all. Now that I am here, I kind of feel like I ran into a wall and I can't figure out how to recover."

"Good to know I make you feel injured," he chuckled and tossed the second bottle in the trash before walking over to sit next to me.

"No, that's not what I meant. You make me feel, I don't know how to explain it. I'm just not sure what my next step should be." Biting my bottom lip and second guessing my words, I waited for him to respond

"You don't need to think so hard about this." He reached over and took the water from my hand. I thought he was going to down it like he had the other two, but he sat it to the side and wrapped my now empty hand in his own. "I wish this felt as natural to you as it does to me. Being with you does something to me. I think the same thing happens to you as well. Only I embrace it, where you seem to want to run from it."

He was right. The last time we were together I ran away from him, back to the safety of my house. It wasn't really him I was running from. I had to get away from 'us' and this bizarre connection we had, but the moment he was close to me again, I looked into his eyes and decided to give in to him and the pull of gray I had been trying to avoid. Heat pulsed through my veins and I could feel it again, that loss of myself. Instead of fighting it I tried to maintain it and enjoy it without letting it override my senses. I focused on his hands, the feel against my own and enjoyed the warmth of his skin, that magical flare of electricity.

Everything slowed and once again the gray was no longer just the shade that rested in his eyes. It was all around us. It escaped him and became an entity of its own filling the room. It blocked out everything and wrapped around us just as it had in the car, only this time I was aware of it, I watched its magic and captured its beauty in my mind. It shielded us giving us protection from the world, nothing else existed. We were all that were.

"Can you feel that?" I didn't want to speak, but the words flowed from my lips regardless.

"What is it that you feel?" His words were heavy and covered in fire, each one landing on my skin and burning right through me. Their touch was not pain. It was raw pleasure in its most pure and simple form. I embraced each one, each impact and allowed them to burn me and leave their imprint on my skin.

"It's all around us; pulsating. Like a heartbeat." I touched his chest with my fingertips. "Like your heartbeat Lacal. Can you see it?" I didn't take my eyes off his. He had to see it. If I focused hard enough, I knew that I would be able to open his eyes to what I was experiencing.

"See?" He didn't see it, but he wasn't confused by my question. "What do you see?"

"Gray," the word flowed from my mouth and spiraled around him. I saw slithers of gray and as they passed his eyes, he was able to see what I saw.

He said no words, he just sighed in awe and grabbed the sides of my seat and pulled me closer to him until our faces were only inches apart. The heat grew between our bodies. "If I kiss you now, do you promise not to run away?" His question was serious, a stern blanket wrapped around his eagerness. He wanted me to say yes, it shot from him like an electric bolt landing in my chest.

"Promise," my body froze and waited for his lips. If I didn't move and didn't breathe, keeping myself planted wouldn't be that hard.

His lips were on mine, soft with gentle urgency. He hesitated and tried to keep his movements restricted. While he was able to maintain his composure, I had failed miserably. I climbed on top of his lap and pulled him into me; my hands once again filled with his hair. He gripped my waist tightly reminding me to reel in my urges.

I pulled away from him slowly and looked into his eyes again; searching for the calming gray I usually found there, but this time as it poured out around me, it was different. It was streaked with pulsating lines of red. Like the blood running through my veins, rushing with adrenaline.

I was beginning to feel more comfortable with this force around us. How it fed off our emotions, our wants and needs and changed itself to mimic that. It was a tangible, visible form of our desires. I was still unsure of where it came from or why I was able to see it. More so, I wondered how I was beginning to understand it.

"I want to try something," I whispered as I climbed off his lap and sat back in my seat. He didn't question me.

We kept our eyes locked; our breathing matched, and as my pulse slowed, so did his. The streaks began to retreat. I took my finger and ran it across his arm slowly. I could feel his pulse quicken; moving the air around us with every beat. This caused the red streaks to grow again, but only a little bit.

I went up his arm and across his chest; checking our shield, pulsing faster, the red growing steadily. I touched his lips then traced the outline of his neck, down to his chest again, it grew even faster. I continued my path down his body. The lower my finger went, the faster it grew and the brighter it got. When I hit the top of his pants, he grabbed my hand.

"Wow!" I looked around seeing how much the red had spread; there was barely any gray left around us.

"What?" He slowed his breath, I hadn't noticed his panting. "What are you doing?"

"Testing a theory," I said as if no further explanation was needed. He looked at me waiting for one.

"Testing? What theory?" He released my hand and stood up.

"You couldn't see the red?" I expected the red to come streaming out and around him like the gray had, but there was nothing.

171

"What red?" This time his control broke and showed his impatience and agitation. He wanted something from me. There was something I was supposed to say or do, and he seemed disappointed that I failed to comply. How could I, when he hadn't told me what it was that he wanted?

"It was like the more excited you became, the redder it got. The red grew and began to replace the gray, like a fire growing and taking over." The connection was broken the moment he stood up, but the shield was still there. I wanted it back more than anything, to experience the effect it had on me. It fueled my body, filling me with primal energy, and I wanted more of it.

"Really?" He walked to the other side of the counter, this time breaking the shield that surrounded us.

"Did I do something wrong?" My mind raced to figure out what I had said or done to incite this reaction from him. I stood from my seat and wanted to tell him to come back but I didn't.

"No," he sighed, "and that's the problem."

"Problem?" I started to walk over to his side of the counter, but he motioned for me to stop.

"Alexa, there is something I need to tell you."

172

Nineteen

He suggested that we move into the living room to continue our conversation. Apparently, whatever we needed to discuss was so bad that cushioned seats would be necessary for me to handle it. Once we were in the living room he didn't say anything. I watched him pace back and forth for nearly ten minutes before his speed slowed and his expression softened from tortured to anxious. I took this as a sign that he was getting closer to telling me whatever it was that he had to say. Abruptly he stopped in front of me as if forcing himself to get on with it.

"Do you remember much about the magic your grandmother used? Did she ever explain anything about it to you?" His question threw me for a loop. What did Nana have to do with any of this?

"No, not really," I tried not to fidget in my seat, but I was uncomfortable.

"Well, that would have made this a lot easier." He sighed and ran his hands through his hair.

"I don't understand. Why would my grandmother's old magic tales have made this easier for

173

you? Are you trying to tell me that you believe in all that stuff?" I looked up at him and tried to find the gray, but something was blocking me. It shouldn't have been so hard to believe, especially now, that I was not only seeing these fields around him, but I was looking for them. Magic was real; I knew it, even if I still chose to try to appear skeptical.

He walked over and sat next to me, close enough for our arms to touch. Staring straight ahead, he lifted my hand from the couch where it sat beside me and held it tightly. Was he trying to hold me there because he was afraid that I would run away from what he had to tell me? Would I want to? What could he possibly say that would be so alarming? So, what if he believed in magic, he wouldn't be the first person I had known to admit that.

"I should start by saying that Jasmine was right when she assumed that I was looking for someone."

"She was?" He avoided my attempt to look him in the eye.

"Yes. I was looking for someone. I was looking for you Alexa." He rushed the words so that he wouldn't lose his nerve. I wasn't sure I had heard him correctly.

"You were looking for me?" It would have had more of an impact, but I had already known. It was the truth that I had just begun to accept.

"Yes. Only I didn't know who you were. This may sound crazy to you, but I have spent the last three

174

years searching for you." He closed his eyes. I should have been concerned about myself, but I only felt protective of him, he seemed so vulnerable.

"You've spent three years looking for me; someone you didn't even know existed? That doesn't make any sense," I tried not to sound judgmental, he needed to finish what he had to say, and I wanted him to because I knew there was more to his story.

"It was what I was born to do. I had no control over it. I exist to be by your side. It's usually a direct link, something inside of us turns on and we are drawn together. That didn't happen. I couldn't feel you and I didn't understand why.

I thought something was wrong with me I figured maybe through the years the bond had been tainted or weakened somehow, but I've never heard of it being so hard. It was my sister who finally pointed out that maybe there was nothing wrong with our bond. She suggested that maybe someone did not want you to be found.

Now that I think about it, that's probably the same reason I couldn't get closer to you that first night. No matter how much I tried to force it, my body just wouldn't move. I begged for my limbs to carry me to you, but nothing happened. It had to be your grandmother's potion that removed the barrier." He looked out the window to the left of the black couch we sat on. My hand was still in his, but the impulse to pull

175

away was not there. Logic said I should want to get away, but I only wanted to be closer to him.

"Okay, wait a minute, back up; you think you were born to be by my side?" My brain screamed for me to run away, but I didn't. I couldn't.

"Yes." I could tell he believed everything he was saying. I wasn't sure if his certainty was comforting or frightening.

"You're serious, aren't you?" Part of me wanted him to laugh and tell me that it was all a joke, but he didn't.

"Please let me explain." Another wave of emotion radiated from him, unhappiness again, this time it hit me harder and stronger. I still couldn't see that field around him, but he was unable to keep everything from me.

"Okay," I couldn't stand to see him so sad, which made about as much sense as the fact that I was still sitting next to him. I barely even knew this guy and what he was telling me should have been setting off warnings that I should get away. Regardless of our attraction, my body should have been on high alert, but it wasn't. I was calm, leaning into him, wanting to hear more. I had accepted his words; I knew there was truth in them even before he said them.

"I am…we are…essentially… from a culture that isn't long lost, or even forgotten, but more like long hidden. Our people aren't exactly from here. By here I mean Earth, this world, or even this universe. The

176

original groups were brought here over 5,000 years ago." His words came out rushed.

"Okay wait a minute," I had to interrupt him at this point. "Say I believe all of this, how and why did 'our people' decide to come here?" Magic was one thing; aliens were a totally different story. Rational thought retuned to me and began to override my physical response to be closer to him.

"It was for the most basic of reasons; sustenance. We live a long time, but in order for our lives to be sustained we have to use the life forces of others. Our planet had a source, but, people got greedy and before long, the natural source was tapped out.

Scouts were sent all over the universe to find other sources. They went from world to world mostly returning home empty handed. The sources they did find were not resilient enough to provide the amount of life force that we required. When they were lucky to find one that was durable enough, they were not very plentiful.

The problem was that most sources, when brought to our home planet, couldn't live very long in our atmosphere no matter what precautions were taken. This wouldn't have been a problem, but combined with their slow reproduction rates, we were taking them out at on average, ten times what they were able to reproduce. Eventually, they would all die off and our people were running out of options.

The scouts were dispatched on what would have been their last search if they came back empty handed. They thought it was over, but then came upon what they described as a line at the edge of the universe. No one knew what it was, so the High Arc was consulted. She demanded that she be taken to this 'line' immediately. Once she arrived she could sense that this was the answer to all their problems. She used her abilities to open it like you would a zipper and on the other side was this world." He paused, and I took a deep breath and tried to process what he had just said. How could I not want to head for the hills, he was basically telling me that I was an alien; or least the spawn of an alien, generations of aliens. Inside I was battling myself, I needed to leave. I didn't want to hear any more.

"So, I assume that this High Arc is like your queen?" I decided to go with it; if he was crazy enough to kill me, I damn sure wasn't going to start provoking him by calling him insane.

"Yes, something similar, only she has no one to answer to, she is ruler of all." His words were filled with an underlying sense of pride and he wanted me to feel it too. He pushed his energy towards me and for a moment I gave in to it.

"I guess that's cool, a woman in charge," I tried to make a joke to ease the tension that was quickly building between us. He was nervous about continuing and I was nervous about hearing more. "So, what exactly were her abilities? I assume that you are saying

178

that she had magical powers?" Tying in my grandmother was starting to make a little more sense now. Maybe he thought there was some connection between her and them.

"Yes. Her abilities were the same as every High Arc. Some of our people are born with maybe one or two basic gifts, like telekinesis, or mind reading, even control over the physical world itself; shaping and molding things to fit their needs.

The High Arc, however, is born with an untold amount of abilities; almost every High Arc has unlocked a new one. The last High Arc, unlocked the ability to cross universes; really one of the most impressive ability I've heard of. All of the abilities once unlocked, are passed on from one High Arc to the next."

"Passed on how?" Something told me I didn't really want to know, but I had to ask.

"Through their blood."

 Twenty

"Their blood?" He couldn't have been talking about blood ceremonies, those creepy rituals you see in movies. That just couldn't be possible. This guy, the one my heart longed for, he believed he was a magical alien who also performed blood rituals!

He looked at me again in that expectant way. The way that said there should be nothing inside of me that questioned what he was telling me. He seemed let down again when I didn't react the way he thought I would. Hell, if my body would have listened, I would have been long gone, running down highway 294 all the way to the safety of my house.

"Yes, all of the High Arcs are related, daughters of daughters." Whew, internal sigh of relief. That made more sense and put a stop to the twisting that was happening in my stomach. When he said it, I felt as if he was still holding something back, something he wasn't quite ready to tell me. This was becoming an annoying pattern with him. Dropping teasers and making me wait for answers. None of which had been delivered yet.

REVITALIZED

"So, she did her magic thing and opened up our universe, then what?" I was interested to know but my curiosity was perched on the borderline of terrified.

"The hunts were successful, obviously. They brought back different species of Earth to test, including a few humans. Some of the other species showed promise, but none quite like humans. They were genetically closer to us than anything else, they even shared similar features. This made them a great source, and they could produce their life force for up to 100 years on our planet if rationed and properly cared for. Combine that with their faster reproduction rates and everything was looking good for both the home world and the humans they had taken.

Each human was fitted with a tap and the sources were distributed to the public. Of course, scientists being scientists, as always, could not leave well enough alone. They continued their testing and figured out that by giving the test subjects some of our life force, we could double, and in some cases, triple their life expectancy.

The only down side was that it did have some negative effects on their reproduction rates. So, scouts were sent again and more humans were taken and distributed to villages, some families even received their own personal tap if they were wealthy enough to pay for them.

To combat the loss of offspring, each woman was scheduled to be mated twice before being treated to extend her life. Hormones were used to produce multiple births. The children were raised and bred. This process was set to repeat, making it possible to replenish the source without having to diminish the entire earth of its people.

On paper this was a great plan, but they conducted ever more research. They didn't want to leave anything to chance. They were determined to make sure that this new source was not sent into extinction like all the others."

"Okay, I'm still not seeing the problem." His explanation was a little long winded, but it sounded like things were good. Okay, so it sounded really freaky, taking humans to breed them and feed from them like cattle. Instead of questioning it, I chose to swallow the bile that those thoughts had created in the back of my throat. "Why did they come here if things were working out so well with the humans on their planet?"

"Shortly after the treated sources were handed out, they discovered that by giving them our life force, it changed their own in more ways than sterilization. It made the sources more potent."

"Potent?" There was a strange feeling in my gut; like I was missing something that should have been painfully obvious, but I was unable to process it. A wall inside my mind was blocking me from understanding it. I did not want to know.

"Yes. It changed the source and whoever drank it changed. They became addicted to it and were unable to control their thirst. A war erupted when the law to ration how much was allowed to be taken was put in place. No one wanted to keep the rations so low. It didn't take long for chaos to spread, and as a result many lives were lost; both humans and our people."

"You keep saying 'our people', but it's sounding like we aren't people at all. I'm starting to think that 'our people' were really cannibals, or as silly as it may sound; vampires." I laughed expecting him to join me, but he didn't. That is when it clicked. The look on his face told me I had hit the nail right on the head.

That was the link that I had overlooked. I knew that was what he was trying to say. He really believed that we were born from alien vampires! I burst into tiny giggles that quickly erupted into full blown laughter.

"That would be the closest definition," his jaw tightened. He stared straight ahead with strained effort refusing to look at me, though I could tell he wanted to. I know I would want to see his reaction if it was me who had just dropped a crazy bomb the size of Manhattan.

"You know, I was willing to listen to all of this because you were sounding so much like my grandmother. Maybe that made me a little nostalgic, but the alien vampire thing is totally new." I couldn't stop laughing. I fanned my face with my hands to cool off my cheeks from the heat of the blood rushing to my face.

"I really wish you would take this more seriously," I could tell he was disappointed by my reaction, but what did he honestly expect me to do? Was

I supposed to admit to having always had a strange craving for blood and ask to be set up with my very own tap?

"I don't know how to do that. You have to understand my position here," I swallowed to stop any more laughter from spewing out. It appeared my brain decided to relay my nerves through a series of snorts and giggles.

"Will you at least listen to the rest of what I have to say?" He finally looked at me. He was showing patience, not seeming at all as irritated as I would have been.

"I have heard this much, I don't see the harm in hearing the rest," I took another deep breath and steadied myself for more, I had no idea what to expect, but from what he had told me so far, it couldn't have been much easier to swallow.

"The mixed blood did something to them. People started to go insane. The scientists were urged to do more testing, find out why this was happening and to fix it. It wasn't long until they realized that people had begun to drink directly from the humans instead of using the taps. The direct intake mixed the blood with the pheromones in the sweat of the humans and made it almost impossible to stop. It led to a lot of humans being drained to their very last drop.

Drinking the last drops of a source had never been a problem in the past, but the mixed blood was different. It was mutated and drinking so much of it at once had an adverse effect. It caused the vampire blood to mutate as well.

They started to change; they became evil, and those who were born with affinities began to use them in unspeakable ways. Instead of improving the world as they usually did, they began to tear it down. They forced their will on anyone who was weaker than they were.

As the numbers of the humans continued to dwindle, people started to demand that more be brought over. The High Arc denied these requests. She refused to cause another source to reach extinction because of the greed of our own people.

Of course, this declaration initiated outrage. The thirst was too much. Eventually they began to attack each other for the remaining humans. When there were no more humans to fight over, they began to feed on each other. It was as if it didn't matter where the blood came from, as long as it made them stronger.

Feeding on each other was the worst thing imaginable; it changed them in a way that proved irreversible. They became stronger, too strong, and it turned out to be something that couldn't be controlled. They became evil in the purest form. It overrode their logic, their wants and desires. It turned them into something dark. One by one it just wrapped around their souls, and shredded them to pieces."

The evil he described reminded me of my dream. The thoughts of that sticky darkness had my entire body covered in goose bumps. That was exactly what I saw and how it felt. The approach of that Darkness, I knew it would devour me, destroy me. He was talking about it figuratively, but it was something literal for me. It had been all around me, moving like it was deliberately coming for me, hungry to rip my flesh from me.

Maybe, I shouldn't be so quick to judge his story. Once again this was too close to home to be coincidence. I wanted to try to take this more seriously and waited for him to continue. All the while logic and emotion raged a war inside my mind.

"After that, an evil erupted that was so horrible that even the High Arc could not control it. Trying to pull them back from their thirst was like fighting an impossible battle. The council pressured her to make a choice. Eventually she did make a decision. There would be a selection of people who would leave our world behind with hopes to return later when those who were left behind had gone extinct. They would attempt to start over."

"The council? I thought she had no one to answer to, where does this council come into play?"

"She doesn't actually. This High Arc was the first to appoint a council. She felt that the people should be able to voice their opinions about the decisions that affected our world. Especially after things started to go dark. She made it clear that she would still have the final say, and all her decisions were final."

"How did she decide? I mean leaving behind so many people to just slaughter each other seems so heartless and cold. That couldn't have been an easy decision for her to make." His answered mattered more than to satisfy my curiosity. I needed to know, my instincts told me that it was important.

"She used one of her abilities, the ability to view auras. It's like what you were doing before. Everyone emits their own field of energy, it tells you their desires, their personality, and it is their essence. By reading their auras she could see who had been corrupted and who was pure."

"I was watching your aura?" I squinted trying to find it again, only there was still a block there. It was coming from him. I felt a physical push on my mind and I tried to push back but it proved to be useless effort as I had no idea what I was doing. He blocked me for a reason, He was hiding something.

"Yes, it's basically a window into the soul. It lets you know what a person is really feeling, what their minds won't allow them to say; it is very useful in determining whether or not someone is lying to you," he said, ignoring the strained expression on my face. We both knew he was keeping me out. Was this because he was lying to me? I frowned and gave up; it would all come to light in time.

"Weren't people mad when they found out what she was doing? I mean, they couldn't have been happy to know that they were being left behind to rot or be slaughtered."

"They didn't know. The entire thing was kept very secret. People only found out after they were recruited and on a ship leaving the planet."

"Still, it had to have been suspicious. People don't just leave for no reason, and without word. How long did it take until they started to realize what she was doing?"

"You are very logical, Alexa." He smiled, almost prideful. "The High Arc was aware of the suspicion this would raise. So, she told her Serve to wait until the last ship was boarded. No one would ever suspect that she would leave him behind. That is exactly why it caused such an upset when she did."

"Her Serve?" He had to stop throwing out terms as if I understood them.

"Yes. This is what I am to you. Each High Arc has a Serve that is born just for them, to be by their side. It is the Serve's duty to guide the High Arc and keep her on the right path. It's also impossible for the High Arc to unlock her full abilities without first bonding with her Serve." He said it like a checklist, something ingrained in his mind.

"Okay...so, how is it possible that she was able to leave him behind? What about their bond? By the way you described it, he was something of a key for her right?"

"Yeah, he was a key for her. Everyone assumed that he was left behind because his aura had been tainted. But it wasn't until after the gateway was closed that they realized it was for other reasons." His expression turned from prideful to somber.

"What other reasons?" I could conceive of nothing that could ever make me want to leave Lacal behind. This was ridiculous! The entire concept of what he was telling me should have been reason enough.

"Once here on earth, Rasmiyah changed our people's appearance. The process was painful because it was done on a genetic level so that their offspring would have the same corrections to their features. There were certain things that needed to be removed, things that were impossible to overlook. Such as elongated ears, eyes without pupils, the coloration of our skin, and our height. A majority of our people grew to more than 8 feet tall.

The High Arc waited for these changes to be made. Then she made an announcement, laws that were to be followed. They were mostly about staying hidden and not giving in to greed. Under no circumstances were humans to be infused with our blood. There would be major consequences to anyone who broke her rules. After she disappeared, it became clear that the reason she left her Serve behind was because she knew that no one would be able to find her without him."

"That was smart." The thought of her leaving her Serve behind made me sick. I couldn't believe she would leave him behind for such a selfish reason. If they were really that connected, wouldn't he just go with her? There had to be more to the story than that. "Wait, so how did the Serve pass on his blood to make future Serves?"

"Serves are not related. It's a random event. This way no one can try to eliminate one before he is able to form his bond with his High Arc."

"I see." Just then, something occurred to me about his story. The High Arcs were supposed to be daughters of daughters who bonded with their Serve in some mystical way that he had yet to explain. He kept referring to the fact that we were supposed to be making this bond. His earlier statement echoed in my mind. '*I exist to be by your side'*. My stomach turned, and the room began to spin. He couldn't be saying what I thought he was. I pushed once more with my mind on the wall he placed between us. The space around him, that energy field, lit up and I knew it was true.

Twenty-One

"You think I'm a High Arc, don't you?" I filled my lungs with air and held it there. I knew what he was going to say, it was impossible to deny it. My hand burned inside of his and something inside me rippled with excitement.

"Yes, I know you are." He believed it. His posture changed when he said it to confirm his convictions. He sat up taller, and pushed his shoulders back, head high.

"Okay," I pulled my hand away from him. "This is crazy. You can't honestly expect me to believe any of this."

I got up and walked away from the couch to the other side of the room. The truth was that I had believed every word. At least up to the point where I became some weird alien vampire queen. That was one announcement that I couldn't accept.

"Why not? It is the truth, Alexa," he followed me across the room. "You've already been experiencing it for yourself. Have you forgotten the party, or the car, or what just happened in the kitchen?" He pointed to the room where I saw the red entangled in gray, the visible proof of his passion for me.

"Okay, so I had a few crazy delusions and lost my self-control once or twice, but that's all very easily explained." It really wasn't, but I could come up with something if I tried hard enough.

"How?" He stared at me, challenging my denial.

"Well, the hallucinations, or whatever they are, were clearly caused by whatever the hell my grandmother gave me, and the self-control...well, it's been a while since I have been that close to someone so attractive. I'm just out of practice, and I overreacted." I rushed to make up more reasons, but even as I spit them out I knew he couldn't believe them. Hell, I didn't believe any of it myself!

"You don't consider the fact that your grandmother gave you a potion that magically healed you as evidence?"

"Yes, I do. It's evidence of magic or science, not evidence that I'm this vampire 'High Arc' that you think you are looking for. It all seems more like coincidence. Besides, I told you about all that the other day, why didn't you tell me all of this then?" I was the one challenging him now.

"I wasn't sure how to," he dropped his head. He was failing to convince me, and it was killing him.

"Don't do that. Please don't," I sighed and lifted his head with my finger, the way he had done to me.

192

"Do what?" He looked at me, trying to figure out what else he had done to let me down and that made me feel even worse.

"Dropping your head, looking so vulnerable; I cann't handle seeing you like that. I don't even know why it affects me so much." I looked away from him avoiding the sad gray clouds that filled the air around us. It hurt to see what he had been hiding, the storm brewing around us.

"I'm sorry, Alexa." He kept his head up and straightened out his facial expression, but the cloud remained.

"Don't be." I turned back to him and placed my hand on his cheek, trying to ease his angst. "I need time, Lacal. This was already too strange to begin with. Then you tell me that I'm basically next in line to be in control of some 'long hidden' culture of vampires! It's not exactly the easiest thing in the world to digest."

"I really am sorry. I know it's a lot. I will take you home now if you wish." He sounded so defeated. It broke my heart to imagine leaving him like that. I didn't want him to beat himself up over me or my decision to run away. This is exactly what he would have done if I decided to leave now.

"No, I don't want to go home." I turned his face to me. I caught one more flicker of gray and then it was blocked again. "I've spent enough time there. Maybe we could hang out here. You can tell me more about you, you know, what you told me we were coming here for."

Inside I was kicking myself for being so foolish. He gave me an out, and I should have taken it.

"What else do you want to know?" He smiled, but the sentiment never touched his eyes; the gray there didn't electrify me like it usually did.

"Anything you want to tell me." He needed to relax, but I wasn't able to get him to.

We sat back on the couch again and he told me about his family. He had a twin sister named, Layal, who looked just like him, only shorter. His mother left home when he was a boy without any explanation. One day she kissed him and walked out the door. He never saw her again. I cried when he told me about her. How could I not? It was his description of the way she looked. His mom and Layal were like twins all their own. It was hard on his father. For months he had alienated Layal because her face would bring him to tears. His father, Lamar, who was an important figure in their community, was the one who trained him after they found out who he was meant to be. Lacal hated it but never asked for another trainer. It was his way of taking his mind off his troubles. It gave him a reason to switch his focus to something else.

He told me about his best friend, Jemal and how everyone was sure he would be the next Serve. Apparently, a witch (yes, there were witches as well) had divined that it would be him. They took this to be truth as her predictions had never been incorrect before. Jemal was trained from birth in the ways of a great

Serve, but on my 17th birthday the connection was triggered, and it was revealed that Lacal was meant to be my serve, not Jemal. He explained that the ceremony took place in the Arc temple where Rasmiyah, a tree attached to the spirit of the mother of 'our people', lived. I thought this was fitting because trees were a considered to be symbols of hierarchy.

When a new High Arc turns 17, the trees leaves begin to glow with a light that comes from Rasmiyah's energy. They don't stop glowing until the Serve to be bonded enters the temple and his blood is offered to the tree, thus stimulating the bond. The bond cannot be completed until both the High Arc and the Serve re-enter the temple together. What happens after that is unknown, as no one else is allowed to witness the event.

"It was like heat, a dull fire racing through my veins. My blood rushed, and I could hear nothing but the sound of your name. I could see nothing but a blurred image of your face. The image was quickly replaced by flashes of Darkness coming for you. It was a warning and I heard it, a thousand voices in one, they told me I had to get to you." He explained it to me as my heart pounded.

When Jemal offered his blood, nothing happened. There of course, was upset and confusion throughout the community. Eventually, one by one, all the boys who were of age lined up to offer their blood. Lacal, was the fifth boy to do so. He described the feeling when the branches bent and reached for him, pouring their light into his soul and connecting him to me forever.

Of course, people were happy because it meant that they were closer to finding their new High Arc, but there were some disappointed that Jemal was not the chosen one. As for Lacal's friendship with Jemal, that was completely over. Jemal didn't appreciate being pushed out of the spotlight. He started to ignore Lacal, and eventually was hanging with people that Lacal thought should be avoided. Jemal wanted the attention back and he was happy with any form of it, even if it was negative.

Jemal was pleased when Lacal left on his search to find me. He figured Lacal's search would be unsuccessful and therefore would never return. He knew that Lacal had too much pride to come back empty handed. This meant Jemal would be able to return to be the golden boy of the village. The last he heard Jemal was basically in charge of the village's security detail.

Lacal was happy to get away from the attention. He wasn't used to it and it bothered him; especially the pressure of finding me. Layal was the one who came up with the theory of something or someone trying to hide me from him. This gave him an excuse to leave, one he was relieved to have. Before this, everyone thought it was best that he sit back and wait for me to come for him or for something to be revealed. They felt that Rasmiyah would show him the way when it was time. This we both now knew would never have happened.

REVITALIZED

"Do you miss them, your father and sister?" That emptiness inside me stung and I tried to focus on Lacal's story and not my own loss. I had done enough moping around about both Nana and my parents. I could suck it up and be there for him.

"Every minute since I left." He grabbed my hand again and held it tightly, always trying to comfort me, he could see right through me, just as I could him.

"You should be happy now." This wasn't about me, it was about him. I wanted to keep the attention where it belonged.

"Why is that?" The look he gave me made me shiver for a moment; this conversation was leading somewhere I was afraid to go.

"You can see your family again now, can't you?" He didn't say anything; he just stared at me with hopeful yet saddened eyes. "I mean you found me and that was what you left home to do. Now you can go back and tell them you succeeded in your quest." It felt weird to think of anyone celebrating over Lacal finding me.

"I suppose so," he dropped his head to stare at the floor with regret in his eyes.

"You don't sound convinced. Don't you want to go back?" My heart skipped a beat, excited that he may choose to stay with me instead.

"I'm not sure if I'm ready to go back to all of that," his shoulders hunched forward. I laid my hand on his back and rubbed it trying to relax him without getting too excited about the contact. It was hard to ignore the way the palm of my hand lit up.

"Why?" I moved my hand to his hair and started stroking his long locks. It was supposed to make him feel better, but the effect it had on me was once again more than I was prepared for.

"I can't lie; it's a lot easier being on my own. There is no stress, no drama, and no politics to deal with. Once I found out who I was, my life was no longer my own. It was theirs, I belonged to the people. I stopped being me and they took over completely. My life became a series of schedules. Training and classes, quizzes and challenges. I had to be prepared; my life was always about preparation. Now, I do what I want, when I want. It's more me and I like it that way."

"I can understand that, but eventually you will have to go back if all you've said is true. They will expect you to return someday."

"You mean *we* will have to return Alexa," He turned and looked at me, and I understood why he had been keeping me out. He was blocking me from his anxiety. This was what he was afraid to tell me, all the other stuff was just so that I would understand. The real reveal was that he couldn't go back unless I went with him.

"What?" I moved away from him. I pulled my right hand from his, my left no longer stroking his hair, just putting that space between us wounded me. The bond tried to pull me back to him, but somehow, I had control. My limbs shouted at me, a new form of agony, not of pain but of want.

"We will have to go back. Alexa, you're the reason I left. I can't go back without you." He stared at me intently.

Throughout his entire speech and even after he told me what he thought I was meant to be, the only thing that had really mattered to me was that he felt okay. I had wanted him to feel like he could continue, because I needed to hear what he had to say. It became my job to make sure he did. I did not stop to factor myself into the equation. He came to me to find me, not just to be my boyfriend and have picnics and long drives together. He came to take me back with him! My chest tightened, I was feeling suffocated, I couldn't tell what was making me feel that way. Was it the pressure of being a queen? Was it the fear of him wanting to take me away? Or the distance I had placed between us? It didn't really matter. I couldn't give him what he wanted.

"I can't." I choked out. I was trying not to hyperventilate or even more embarrassing, pass out. I took deep breaths trying to sooth the burning that was now growing in my chest.

"Why?" He whispered the question. He was afraid and so was I, but for two entirely different reasons. He feared that I would say no. I feared that I would want to say yes.

"I don't know...I just can't." I shook my head trying lift the weight of the decision he was asking me to make.

"You have nothing here, anyway," his words were sincere and patient, but they still managed to burn like lava on my skin.

"And that means what? Am I supposed to pick up and follow you, a complete stranger, to only God knows where?" I got up. I had to get away from him, so I could think clearly. He looked at me and I felt myself giving in, but, there was no way I could give him this. That irrational, impulsive, animalistic side of me would give Lacal the world, but the logical, self-preserving side, told me that this was too much to give. He had no right to ask it of me.

"You have to accept this." He pleaded with me, but I ignored him and the angst that his words caused me to feel.

Putting up my own wall was easy now with this anger inside of me, just as it had been with my grandmother. Everyone I loved, I couldn't keep. I did love Lacal, deep down. It simmered within me and every time he came near me, the heat came closer to the surface. However, that no longer mattered because I would never be able to give him what he wanted. He would leave, just like she did.

"I don't have to accept anything. You are out of your mind. I don't even know you and you're asking me to leave the only life I have, and run off to some imaginary world with you!" My words hurt him, but it was how I felt, and I had to defend myself against the choice I knew he would make.

"Alexa…" He wanted to continue to try and convince me, and he would have if I had let him keep talking.

"No. No more. I'm going home. Now!" I brushed him off and refused to look at him; if I did I would cower instantly. There was only so much resolve I was capable of with him and the limit was quickly approaching.

"Okay, I'll get my keys." He gave up his fight and turned to the kitchen where he had tossed them on the counter.

"Don't bother, I'll call Jazz and have her pick me up," being in the car with him wasn't a good idea. It wasn't that I didn't trust him. Lacal would do whatever I wanted him to, I knew that. I couldn't trust myself. In the closed space of the car, I would definitely lose my bearings and be taking off to space land with him.

I grabbed my jacket and purse from where I had tossed them on the arm of the couch and headed for the door.

"Where are you going to go?" He sounded more protective than angry, but I did not turn around to see if his expression confirmed that. Just like with Nana. I didn't want him to be angry, but there was only so much of myself I could give.

"We drove by a coffee shop; it wasn't that far away, I'll wait for her there."

"Don't be ridiculous! You can stay here and wait. I won't bother you," he was telling the truth, but it didn't matter. He jumped in my path.

"Now, I'm being ridiculous? I'm not staying here," I sounded like a child throwing a temper tantrum as I refused to cooperate or listen to reason, but getting away from him was the only thing on my mind. It was the only way to be sure I would not do anything irrational.

He stopped protesting. He knew that I wouldn't be changing my mind. At least not right now. Keeping my head down, I pushed past him. The door was heavier than I thought, and it fought against my efforts to open it. Lacal reached around me and easily pulled it open, which only irritated me more. I pushed the door aside, stepped out, and with all of my effort slammed it behind me.

He didn't follow me and that part inside of me that was bonded to him, cried in disbelief. If he thought we were meant to be together for all of eternity, why didn't he fight harder to keep me there? Why didn't he demand that I listen to him and refuse to let me walk out of that door? Why did he give up so easily?

Twenty- Two

While I walked to the coffee shop, I called Jazz who wasted no time in drilling me with questions. Not only was I not in the mood to answer, I didn't know what to say. I interrupted her but promised to answer her questions later. I had no idea how to put what happened into words without making it sound like I was completely insane or that Lacal was. After all that I really was starting to feel like I had lost a few marbles.

I believed him. Against my better judgment and as hard as I tried to override my emotions with logic I believed him. It all seemed impossible. His words touched me in a way I had no explanation for. They reached inside me and felt more real than anything I'd ever heard before. The truth was simply undeniable.

The little shop was further away than I remembered. Walking past the duplicate houses felt like being in a cartoon scene. I pictured myself as Fred Flintstone chasing after Barney Rubble. It always irritated me how the images in the background never changed. No matter how long they ran, they never made it out of that damn room! I chuckled to myself and was glad for the momentary release.

I made it to the coffee shop and was relieved to find it empty. Crowds made it impossible to think with the added chatter. I would end up doing more people watching than thinking about my own issues. I ordered my drink and grabbed a table by the window facing the parking lot to give me a clear view of Jazz when she showed up.

"Here you go, do you need anything else?" The waitress handed me the tea I ordered and stood there bouncing the pencil eraser on her notepad.

"No, I'm alright." I expected her to walk away but she didn't. "Can I help you with something?"

She just stood there and looked at me for a moment. She looked tired but not from lack of sleep, more like she had been out the night before and was still hung over. Her blond hair was thrown into a sloppy ponytail that was barely holding on. The name tag that was pinned crookedly on her brown polo that all the waitresses wore read, Lauren.

Her pants, which hung from her skinny waste and sagged to her hips, had stains on them that I hope were from work related spills. Her shoe laces were untied, an obvious hazard for a waitress. All in all, she looked like she could use a shower and about 12 hours of sleep.

"I just wanted to see what all the fuss was about," she tilted her head, rolled her eyes and turned to walk away.

"Excuse me?" She turned back to me, "Fuss about what?"

"You," she pointed her finger and me and smiled.

"Me? What are you talking about?" I hate to admit it, but I was already irritated with her.

"You did just walk here from that guy Lacal's house, right?" The window gave a clear view of the path back to Lacal's place. She must have seen me coming.

"So?" I didn't like her saying his name, our bond made me territorial, and if she said one negative thing about him I would probably attack her.

"This is a very small part of town. I got about 20 texts before you even hit the door. You've pissed off a lot of girls. This little town is like a restaurant. Lacal, as we see him, is a new customer. Wouldn't you be mad if a fresh customer came into your establishment, sat down, and asked for takeout?" She rolled her neck and sucked her teeth.

"Did you just call me takeout?" My patience had already been tried after dealing with Lacal's revelation, and now my fuse was short, barely there. I pushed my seat from the table and stood up, ready to fight. My body needed to release endorphins and she had just given me the perfect way to do that.

Lauren smiled at first, ready for a fight. She dropped her right leg back, and put up her fist, and stood in a boxing stance. I should have stopped and second guessed my decision. Hell, I was no trained fighter, barely a scrapper, but my anger had taken over again. When I was angry, I was invincible, or least my mind thought I was.

Something about her changed after I stood up completely. Her brown eyes went from cocky to terrified. I almost turned to see what was behind me that could possibly be so distressing, but she wasn't looking behind me, she was looking at me.

"What? Why are you looking at me like that?" I stepped closer to her; she jumped backward and stumbled into the table behind her. I saw her aura then, she was terrified of me. The colors were frantic. It was something I hadn't expected from this girl. I imagined the girl to be bossy, pushy, and sometimes overbearing.

"I'm sorry, I didn't mean to...I didn't know," awkwardly she raced away from me into the back of the shop behind the counter. She tripped before she made it there and nearly hit her face on the counter.

Maybe, I should have asked her what she meant, but after speaking to Lacal, I realized ignorance was truly bliss. I sat back in my chair and started sipping the mint tea I had ordered. I looked over my shoulder once and caught her staring at me. She freaked when I looked at her and retreated behind the counter again, pretending to be busy with inventory. But there was something there, recognition. Inside I felt that entity unravel and purr as if it were proud. I drank more tea, trying to drown it out.

After I shook off the incident with the waitress and relaxed, my mind belonged to him again. How could something feel so right and at the same time make absolutely no sense at all? Everything about Lacal just screamed that he belonged with me. His presence called something inside of me to life. I already felt protective of him, even though he was probably more capable of protecting himself than I was. With him it was all instinct; so much easier to be free and not worry about how everything else in my life had been so messed up.

Time passed faster than I wanted it to. I needed more time. Jazz would want an explanation for why she had to drive two hours to come get me. There would be no stopping her until she was satisfied. My stomach began to ache as I realized there was no way that I could possibly satisfy her.

I saw the red convertible pull up in front of the shop about a second before she blew the horn. I grabbed my stuff, chugged down the rest of my drink and headed out to face the music. Lauren stood by the door, and as I approached, backed away slowly to give me space. She looked almost like she was bowing, and I would have dismissed the idea, but when I walked by her I heard her say it. *'Your Highness'* it was a whisper, barely audible, but I heard it, I stopped and stared at her for a moment. Inside I was moved, I could feel every part of me spring to life as I heard her, it felt right. She looked at me with eyes wide with awe and smiled shyly. I swallowed my pride, smothered the feelings that were arising, and continued out the door.

I had barely sat down in Jazz's car before she fired away.

"What happened? Did he get grabby with you? You know I will kill him if he did!" She threw the car into drive and sped out of the parking lot. If it hadn't been empty, she would have killed someone.

"No," I clutched the door handle.

"So, what happened?" She demanded.

"Nothing, he just wants more from me than what I can give him," I stared out of the window trying to avoid more questions.

"Like what, sex?" She sounded mad and it made me smile, though I hid it from her. I really had missed her acting like my defensive older sister.

"No," if only it was that simple. "He wants me to go away with him."

"Go away?" She paused. "So, go." She shrugged.

"What?" I turned to her, my mouth hanging open.

"I mean what's a little weekend away? You could use a vacation from Drabville, USA." She stuck her tongue out at me.

"I don't think it was only a weekend he had in mind." I picked up my jaw.

"Seriously?" She didn't sound as shocked as I thought she should have.

"Yes, he feels we are meant to be together and I should go live with him," I tightened my grip on the door handle as she dipped in and out of traffic causing the car to swerve wildly."

"That's a lot after only knowing you for less than a week?" Still there was something in her tone, almost as if she was faking her responses.

"Yeah, I know, it's way too much." I ignored the twisting inside me that was telling me it wasn't too much.

"Wow. No wonder you ran away." She was looking at the road much too intensely. Jazz was never the severely cautious driver. She usually slouched and rarely glanced ahead. Too distracted by all the gadgets she kept with her.

"I did not run away." I sighed. Okay, so yeah, I did. Again.

"What exactly would you call it?"

"I simply chose to remove myself from a stressful situation. You know kind of how I wish I could remove myself from your terrible driving right now. It was the healthy thing to do." I stuck my tongue out at her mimicking her own behavior.

"You could always walk," she laughed and pulled onto the expressway and hit the gas, accelerating much more than was necessary. "Healthy huh, well I say it's the same thing. So?"

"What?" I chewed my lip and watched the blur of cars that passed the window.

"Why not?"

"Why not what?" I looked at her this time as she sucked her teeth.

"Why not go with him?" She did not turn to face me; the road was just too captivating.

"You can't be serious. You just agreed that it was too soon for all that."

"It's not like you can't come back if it doesn't work out." The truth was I probably couldn't come back home, but I didn't want to tell her that.

"I can't believe this! A few years of solitary, and I come out to a completely different Jazz. You're insane if you think this is okay."

"I'm no different. It is not insanity; it is called having an open mind." She nodded her head and winked at me over the red shades she wore.

"Yeah…right," I couldn't ever remember Jazz being remotely open-minded. Jazz was routine, things should go a certain way, and she would always stick to that. Her entire existence was scheduled and planned. Now she was suggesting that I abandon all strategy and logic and run away with a stranger.

"What?" She sighed; I couldn't believe she was disappointed that I wasn't on board with this.

"Are you telling me that you would go with him?"

"Um…"she couldn't say she would because we both knew she'd be lying.

"Exactly, you're so daring and open minded, but only when it's not your life."

"I'm not the one who needs a little excitement."

"That would be more than a little. I mean going with him, it could be the end of my life. I don't know. What if he is some serial killer collecting sickly girls that no one will miss?"

"Don't be so dramatic. I'm telling you if he wanted to hurt you, he would have done it by now." I couldn't see her eyes through the shades, but, I knew she was rolling them at me. "I mean, he definitely wouldn't have just let you go if his plan was to murder you. Besides, I would miss you Lex!"

"I guess you're right," she was, I knew it, as inexplicable as it was, I did know it. Lacal would never hurt me, he couldn't.

"Look the only thing that matters is if you think he is dangerous. If you do, then of course you should listen to your instincts. Do you?" This time she turned to me. She wanted me to change my mind. Why?

"I'm not sure. It's like a part of me says no, but I can't make it fit. It doesn't make sense." I bit my lip and stared back out of the window.

I needed to think and was relieved that Jazz let me. We drove the rest of the way to my house in silence. I debated how much she needed to know. Her opinion of the situation wouldn't be the same once she knew everything he had told me. It couldn't. She would tell me to stay away and probably have him hauled off in a strait jacket.

I didn't want to invite her in and appear desperate for her company. I needed my friend, but was starting to feel clingy. Thankfully, it wasn't necessary to ask. When we pulled up to my house, she put the car in park, shut off the engine, and hopped out.

This is why we had always been best friends. She could sense when I needed her and though it occurred far less often, I could sense when she needed me. Once again it was a comfort to find that some things hadn't changed with time.

We made a beeline for the kitchen, grabbed snacks, and went up to my room. Jazz snatched the body pillow from the floor in front of my bed and curled up with it. We chose my *Sex and the City* box set and put the first disk in.

For a while we were back in high school. We curled up together under the covers dipping Doritos in sherbet ice cream. (Yes, I am aware of how gross it sounds, but it's actually delicious.) We washed it all down with coke while reciting the words to every episode before the characters even had a chance to say them. We used to argue over which characters we were. Finally, after many extensive debates, we decided that she was a Samantha/Miranda combination and I was a Carry/Charlotte combination, two walking contradictions.

REVITALIZED

After the first DVD finished playing, we sat for a while looking at old pictures and talking about events I had missed out on. There were parties and fights, break-ups and make-ups, and college drop-outs that were completely expected and one that was not. Even a girl who decided she wasn't a girl at all, and elected to have a sex change. Jazz claimed she knew even when we were in high school, but I found that hard to believe because she constantly tried to hook her up with the basketball players.

"He thinks I am a vampire queen!" There was a lull in the conversation and I blurted it out. It was the only way I could say it out loud that wouldn't make me lose my nerve.

"What? You mean Lacal?" She nearly choked on the coke she was chugging down.

"Yep," I rolled on my side to look her in the face.

"Okay, spill," she mimicked me, propping her head on her hand.

I told her everything. I included all the unbelievable and inexplicable things that had happened from the first encounter all the way up to the auras in his kitchen and the confession in his living room. For the first time ever, Jazz was completely speechless. No witty remarks or quick come backs. She stared at me blinking while I waited for her response. I couldn't read her. Jazz always had the greatest poker face. She had to have been thinking how insane it all was and was just trying to put it into words.

"Say something," her silence was heavy. It poured from her and affected my own voice. I could barely push myself to speak up. She was thinking something and I wasn't sure if it would be good to find out what it was.

"Go." She said simply, one word, nothing more, complete insanity.

"What?" I sat up. My ears had to have been deceiving me.

"You have to." She looked at me like she was both nervous and excited about the advice she was giving me.

"What are you talking about?" I adjusted the pillow behind my back which had begun to cramp from lying in the same position for so long.

"Come on, after everything you told me between you and him, I mean even your grandmother is tied into this. Don't you want to find out why? Don't you want to know if all this is true? Maybe you can find out where your grandmother went."

"You're serious, aren't you?" Giving up on the pillow, I sat against the head board, wrapped my arms around my legs and rested my head on my knees.

"Yes." She sat up next to me pushing aside the hair that fell into my face.

"How? How can you say that Jazz?"

"Lex, you have been given, in an odd way, an opportunity most people dream of; a new life, a new adventure. Why wouldn't you want to take advantage of that?"

"This is not at all what I expected from you." I tilted my head to look at her and hoped that I would find her smiling jokingly, but I didn't.

"What did you expect?" She sighed and paused. "Okay, to be honest, and I have to be honest here, Lacal has already talked to me about this. Yes, I reacted the same way that you did. I'm sure you freaked out, but he showed me things. Things I can't even begin to explain, but you have to know, if I didn't believe him, there is no way I could have sent you there."

"You knew?! Why didn't you tell me? Jazz, how could you do that to me?"

"What did I do Alexa? I listened, I believed and even though you are having trouble admitting it, I think you do too."

"I just…I can't believe this, talking to you was supposed to offer me a logical side, a way out of it. Now you are rooting for him."

"Well, what do you want from me? I am just telling you the truth; that's all I can do."

"I don't know, an easy way out maybe? I mean, vampire queen? Even if it all wasn't crazy enough, toss that into the mix. Am I supposed to just accept this huge weight as if it's nothing?" I tightened my arms around my legs. This wasn't the type of comfort she was supposed to be giving me.

"Alexa, my sister, my best friend, if you want out, then get out. You don't need me for that. Something is telling me it isn't that simple is it?" She wrapped her arms around my shoulders, I needed support, and she wanted to give it to me. She knew that the advice she gave me wasn't what I wanted, but it was exactly what I needed.

"No, I really don't think it is." I cried and she wiped my tears away.

We talked for a while about anything that did not concern Lacal, I needed to get him out of my head, and Jazz knew that. She tried to help me distract myself, unfortunately that never actually happened. After a while it was time for Jazz to go, I didn't want her to, but she had other things to do. She gave me a hug and told me she supported me no matter what choice I made. That made me feel better, even though I had no idea what I was going to do. If by chance I did decide to do something completely irrational, it was nice to know my friend was by my side.

I retreated to my room and lay in my bed staring at the ceiling. The cracks somehow looked different; as if they had changed. I peered at them trying to figure out what was different, not one pattern or web looked familiar. I studied them until I fell asleep with thoughts of change lingering in my mind.

Twenty-Three

The dreams I had that night were different than the previous nights. Instead of clear images, my friends or my room, it started off as just random flashes of crooked smiles and smoldering gray eyes that gave me a feeling of happiness and safety. They also made me feel powerful. His voice echoed in my head; calling my name playfully. All of the uncertainties I had before were erased by the calm deep melodic timbre of his voice.

Finally, he materialized in front of me; shirtless and smiling. His hair flowed around his face moving in dark waves. He opened his arms to me and I ran into them, hard enough to knock him over, but he barely flinched. As our bodies collided, he captured my lips in a kiss and I felt as if I would melt. My legs turned to into jelly and had it not been for his arms wrapped tightly around me, I would have hit the ground.

He whispered my name into my ear and the sound of it did things to my body I had never experienced before. Biological responses firing off and leaving my skin tingling. I smiled and kissed his shoulder covering it in tiny little pecks, each one lingering for just a moment. I wanted him, he belonged to me and nothing else mattered.

Reluctantly waking up from my dream, I picked up the phone and dialed his number. There was nothing to think about anymore. He answered on the first ring sounding breathless, as if he had just been out for a run. I pushed away the images of his sweat covered flesh. I bit my lip and waited for him to speak.

"Alexa?" The breathy way he said my name made my heart race.

"Yes." I bit down harder onto my bottom lip with enough force to draw blood.

"What's wrong?"

"Nothing why?" I scanned the room, there was nothing wrong. I just needed him; I wanted him near me.

"I felt your heart racing; it woke me from my sleep." He cleared his throat, but I would have preferred if he hadn't. There's nothing sexier than the sound of a man's voice when he just wakes up. That scratchy, gruff sound that covers their already deep tone, it was hypnotic, an aphrodisiac.

My cheeks burned. I wasn't sure if he knew what I was dreaming about, but I did know he felt it. That alone was enough to make me embarrassed. Not to mention that I was now imagining him shirtless, lying on his bed covered in sweat. My heart was still racing. Could it still be sending him messages? Would he realize it meant something much different than fear, that I was excited and not afraid?

"It's nothing. I was just dreaming, don't worry. You felt my heart? Wow!" I rambled on to steer the conversation in a direction that would slow the pace of my heart. It was amazing, the connection we had, how could I have wanted to run from it?

"Yes, I did. Your heart is my heart Alexa," he breathed deep and sighed. "Are you sure you're okay?"

"Yes, Lacal, I am fine. Please relax; I think I can feel your heart too." The moment I said it I knew it was true. Slowly, I felt his deep breaths he was now taking, reach across our connection to help calm my own pulse and wished I was with him, to inspire my heart to go off on another race.

"Good. So why did you call? I was sure you would never want to speak to me again." He said with a defeated quality to his voice.

"I called because," I bit my lip chewing on the words, holding back now would be pointless; he would be able to feel it. "I want to see you Lacal, I need to see you."

"You do?" He was reasonably confused by my confession. "Are you sure everything is okay?"

"Yes. Everything is great. You don't have to sound so shocked," I joked to make light of the situation.

"Like I said, I figured I would never get to see you again." He gave a small laugh, one of relief. He sighed, and I felt his breath on my neck.

219

"Well you will if you still want to." It was possible that he would not want to be around me again. Especially with his new-found love of life alone on the road. He wanted to avoid drama. I was now the queen of all things drama.

"Of course, I do." He responded as if he couldn't believe I would think otherwise.

"Good, come over." I meant for it to sound more like a question than a demand.

"Now?" He was already moving, noise of fabric rustling in the background.

"Yes. Please," I didn't want to order him around, but I was excited to see him, to be near him.

"Okay, I'm on my way." He hung up the phone and I sat there for a while, my body tingled all over. I was eager to be with him again and he was coming to me.

I decided to freshen up. My dreams had left me sweaty and breathless, and I wanted to look my best when he arrived. Besides, Lacal was protective and a bit paranoid. If I came to the door looking like I had been running from someone, he would be ready to fight to defend me against harm. Damn that was sexy!

I took a shower and found some new clothes to wear, nothing special, sweats and an oversized T-shirt. Looking like I was anxious to have him at my house in the middle of the night would be bad, even if I was pacing back in forth waiting for him.

REVITALIZED

Lacal arrived less than an hour after he hung up. He had to have been seriously breaking the speed limit. I told myself I would play it cool but the second I heard the car door slam shut and his footsteps approaching my door, I could not contain myself. I flung the door open before giving him a chance to knock like any normal person would have done. I pulled him inside and started kissing him hungrily. I heard the door shut, he must have kicked it closed, because his arms were already wrapped around me and carrying me through the hall.

The world spun out of control as my back made contact with the wall. I threw my head back as he nibbled my neck and kissed my collar bone. I giggled as his tongue danced across my skin in small spirals. I said his name just moments before his lips took hold of mine and we were moving again. My legs wrapped around his waist as he carried me into the living room.

He placed me down on the couch and for a moment, leaned on top of me and let the kiss deepen. A guttural moan came from within me, muffled by our lips that were still pressed tightly together. I grabbed at him harder, pulling him into me, so much for playing it cool.

My hands busied themselves with undressing him, while my legs tightened around his waist pulling him closer to me. Every part of my body worked in a separate but unified effort to feed the dying flame my dream had left behind.

He was just as captivated, pulling me closer, running his hands through my hair. He kissed me like he would never be able to again; ciphering off as much of me as he could. I arched my body up, offering myself to him, wanting to give him all of myself. Then he stopped. Damn it, I couldn't believe it, but he stopped.

"Wait," he pulled away from me, pressing his back to the other end of the couch.

"What? Did I do something wrong?" I started to move toward him, but, he put his hand up to me telling me to stop.

"No," he laughed roughly. "Trust me, you did nothing wrong, but all of this is a bit confusing Alexa."

"I'm sorry; I didn't realize how late it was when I asked you to come." I sat back against my side of the couch and began straightening out my clothes. My cheeks were turning red with embarrassment.

"Its fine," he moved closer to me and took another deep breath. "So why did you want me to come? Or did I just foolishly interrupt the reason you wanted me to come?" He tried to make a joke to get rid of the tension, but only succeeded in making me feel more self-conscious.

"No, I just wanted to let you know my decision and I thought it would be better if I did it in person and not over the phone." I looked down at my fidgeting fingers.

"Your decision, what decision?" He held his breath, he already knew what I had chosen to do he just needed to hear the words.

"Yes, I'm going."

"Going where?" Still, he needed me to say it.

"With you, to your village," I rolled my eyes at him. Where else could I possibly be talking about going that would require me to tell him about in person?

"What made you change your mind?" He grabbed my hands to take my attention away from my fingers, and bring me to him.

"I don't know. In a way it was you, I guess. There aren't that many good things going on in my life and, as irrational as all of this is, you make me happy. There is no explanation for it, but, we are connected in some way that's deeper than my wanting to rip your clothes off every time I am near you. Whatever that connection is, I can't risk losing that."

"I hoped that you would change your mind, but you have to know that you wouldn't have lost me, Alexa. I am bound to you. I can't simply walk away, that is not an option for me, not unless the bond is severed." He grabbed my hand again and looked at me. He was happy, proud and it made me want him more. That he could look at me and see someone so worth leaving everything behind for. He believed in me even though he knew so little about me.

Twenty- Four

Lacal took his time with walking me through a step-by-step guide of what to expect after we left. He warned me that it would be a lot to take in. On top of the culture shock, we had a long trip to his village and the events that would occur after we arrived would be overwhelming. He explained the process we would have to go through to solidify our bond. At least he explained as best as he could be considering no one had ever seen it done, it was just speculation passed along by word of mouth. We would have to offer ourselves to Rasmiyah together; this is how she would seal our bond and help me unlock whatever abilities I possessed.

We had only a few days before we needed to leave. Now that I had chosen to accept my new life, the tree would send off a signal to notify the people and they would expect us. If we didn't show up, they would send out a search party. Even though he could sense the panic building inside of me, I still tried my best to hide it from him. As terrified as I was of everything I was walking into, I didn't want him to know it. He assured me that everything would be fine and that there was nothing to worry about.

After I reigned in my nerves enough to stop my thoughts from spiraling away from me, we started preparing to leave. I called Jazz and told her about my decision and that we would have to make a quick departure. She of course, was sad that I would be leaving, we had only just reunited and now I was taking off, but she also seemed happy about my decision to choose a new life. She promised to look after my house and to revamp (yes, she used that ridiculous pun) my wardrobe, even though I begged her not to. She asked how long I would be away. I looked to Lacal who had no real answer for her. He dodged it skillfully. He told her that I would be able to keep in contact and eventually come back to visit.

I packed my warmest clothes, because he said I would need them, but he was very vague about the exact destination as if he feared someone was listening in. After he looked at my inadequate selection, he shook his head, and went to the store to buy more. I told him it was unnecessary, but he insisted, vowing that I would thank him for it later. I couldn't help but notice that even though he didn't ask for my size, everything he bought fit me perfectly.

The following two days consisted of random shopping trips. Apparently, I needed a lot more than new coats and sweaters. He laughed as the list grew longer, repeatedly poked fun at me, and asked how I survived before he arrived. We packed my things, cleaned, and secured the house. Jazz came over to say goodbye multiple times, and to threaten Lacal's life. She said she would hunt him down and kill him if anything bad happened to me. Considering what I knew about Lacal, that was close to impossible, but I appreciated her effort.

Lacal cooked for me; it seemed, he had missed his chance to do so because of my storming out of his house. I doubted that he was really planning to cook for me; it seemed more like an excuse to get out of helping me clean. I appreciated a good meal, so I let him off the hook. He made chicken with corn and rice. A simple meal, something I would have made for myself, but he did it well. He used a honey-lemon glaze with a seasoning he told me was a chef's secret. It was his mother's recipe, and he had promised not to tell anyone. I thought about my mother's pancakes and hated that I would never be able to say the same.

"What do you know about these carvings?" He ran his finger along the table, tracing the design engraved in the wood.

"The carvings? They were a hobby of my dad's. He spent years creating them all over the house."

"Interesting," He popped another piece of chicken into his mouth.

"Interesting? Why is that?" I took over tracing the pattern with my finger. I thought of my father and smiled.

"These are cloaking spells. I didn't recognize them at first but I have seen them before. It's something often used to hide something or in this case, someone." He sat back in his chair and stared at me.

"What do you mean?" I stopped tracing them and thought about his words.

"Well, you were hidden from me Alexa. That's why I couldn't find you. This house is a fortress."

I chose not to respond. If what he said was true, it meant my father was in on the deception as well. My life had just been flipped upside down, just when I was beginning to feel normal again. I couldn't bear adding one more thing to my list of heartaches, especially not my father's name. We spent the night together. Well, I should say he slept over, me in my room and him in the guest room. This was my last night at home for what would be an undetermined length of time. I would miss my house, but I found comfort in knowing that it would still be there for me whenever I needed it.

On the second night, the night before we would leave, we slept downstairs on the couch and talked more about the trip, my nerves, and what was going to happen. I fell asleep with my head on his shoulder and woke up lying on the couch with him behind me, his arms wrapped around me; making waking up in my own home that last morning, one that I would never forget.

The sun pierced through the curtains announcing that it was nearly time for us to go. I took the chance to walk around one last time taking mental pictures in my mind, memories of home. Lacal took my bags to the car, and checked for the hundredth time, to make sure that we hadn't forgotten anything.

"Are we going to get your stuff?" I noticed he wasn't loading anything for himself.

"No need to, I already have my stuff." He smiled and opened the car door for me to get in.

"When did u get it? You didn't leave for that long yesterday." I sat in the passenger seat and looked back at him before he closed the door.

"I told you, I knew you were going to change your mind." He closed the door and walked around the front of the car with the most satisfied look I'd ever seen on his face.

The trip to Lacal's village was bewildering. I tried to focus so I'd remember the way, but I couldn't. The most I could decipher was a confusing series of random twists and turns. The ride seemed to take forever, we had already been in the car for 12 hours, and I was ready for it to be over. I drifted in and out of sleep even though I wasn't tired. I made no complaints though, sleeping helped to pass the time.

My questions were endless; about where we were going, and what I had missed during my naps, but all he would say was that it would be easier to explain once I was trained to know what to look for. His village had no name only a number, 719; my birthday. He said it was prophesied that it would be the day I was born, though the year was unknown. Apparently, the prophet was correct. All the villages were named the same, different dates for different Arcs, I was apparently the first to accept the position, but many had been born before me. Great! That doesn't make a girl second guess herself!

All the Vampire questions had been asked before we left. You know the ones that dispute the standard vampire image on television and in movies. Why he didn't burst into flames in the sun, I also hadn't seen him drink any blood, but I figured that was because we really hadn't spent that much time together. He laughed at me, which basically made me want to punch him, but I got over it. He said he would tell me more about it later.

Sunlight didn't affect all vampires. There were two types of vampires, two opposite sides. His side was the side of Light. The sun did no harm to them and actually decreased their need to drink blood but it was still a necessity. They fed off the energy of the sun. He did drink blood, but only about once a week and that would only change if he exerted too much energy. He said when he used to play sports, before he found out he was meant to be my Serve, he needed about three a feeds week. While he was in training, to learn to protect me, it was so strenuous and intense that he needed to feed daily.

The other side of the coin was Darkness. This side consisted of the vampires who chose to go against the rules set by the High Arc. Once it became clear that she was essentially gone for good, they began to feed from the humans more than was allowed. This eventually led to infusions which of course changed their souls like the people of their home planet. Darkness took them over and the sun, like light to dark, became their enemy.

Only the vampires who chose Darkness had fangs. This was because they fed directly from the humans and their bodies evolved to fit their new lifestyle. They were horrible, wicked looking things. Not the classic long, pointy canines in the movies; there were ten of them, six on top and four below. They were designed to kill, not to please. The vampires on the side of Light used taps, which were basically needles with tubes attached, or blood banks, but in a pinch, they could use their nails to puncture the humans before feeding. This was a riskier method, if not done carefully there was a chance of the blood mixing with the pheromones in the skin which was exactly what caused a vampire to go dark.

The problem with the dark vampires had been kept under control only because the people knew what to look for and how to deal with it. They were contained early in their change. Most of the ones who chose to rebel were banished. The more substantial offenders, the ones who had attempted to harm the order of things, were killed.

After my Awakening, a process that all vampires who are born and not created had to go through; I would need, want, and crave blood. I cringed at the idea of drinking another person's' blood, but it was something I had assumed would come into play at some point.

The Awakening was a ceremony that crossed a person over into their new life as a full vampire. Vampire newborns were given a serum that would subdue their true nature. That side of them remained dormant until this ritual was performed to awaken it. This was something that only happened on earth. It was implemented through the powers of the spirit of Rasmiyah in the High Arc temple to allow them to blend in better. Before they came here a vampire was a vampire by all accounts from the moment they were born. On Earth there were rules and standards, such as children going to school, that needed to be kept intact.

Full vampire children in school with human children would only bring unwanted attention and would ensure the extinction of either the humans or the vamps. I was behind on my Awakening, by nearly eight years, so the process would have a stronger effect on me. That was the last thing he said before I slipped off into another nap.

When the car finally stopped we were no longer in Chicago. That much was obvious, between the amount of time that had passed and the frozen land that spread out around us. When we left Chicago it was 75 degrees, now the digital thermometer on his dashboard read only 5!

As to where we were, I had absolutely no clue and didn't really care. I embraced the chance to be out of the car and able to stretch my legs. I stepped out of the car onto the snow-covered ground and wanted to hop right back in. Stretching could wait! My bones chattered from the arctic air that slammed against my body. He was right about me wanting to thank him for getting me warmer clothes.

"Where are we?" I rubbed my arms with my hands, and my teeth chattered.

"Antarctica." He slammed the door and checked to make sure it was locked. As if there would be anyone showing up to steal it in the middle of Antarctica!

"What? That is impossible. There is no way to drive from Chicago to Antarctica! We were in the car the entire time, and as far as I can tell, your car didn't grow wings." I followed him to the back of the car.

"No, my car did not grow wings," he laughed and shook his head at me.

"So how do you explain this?" I waved my arms around me at the emptiness surrounding us.

"Portals," he opened the trunk and handed me a large blue coat.

232

"What?" I pulled the coat on and quickly zipped it up as far as it would go. The thick insulation helped to warm me up quickly.

"We use portals for travel. It's faster and it helps to keep us more separate from humans." He pulled out a smaller jacket for himself and pulled it on.

"I didn't see any portals," I scanned the area around us searching for them, but I wasn't exactly sure what I was supposed to be looking for.

"How would you know?" He laughed at me again, clearly enjoying himself. "Have you ever seen a portal? Do you know what one looks like?" He vocalized my own thoughts.

"Well, no. I don't, but…" I scratched my head, and the disorientation settled in.

"Exactly, so how would know you if we had used them?" He put on a light jacket, apparently not as affected by the cold as I was.

"I guess I wouldn't." I conceded, but still scanned the area.

"It's not like Star Trek or any of the other Hollywood versions you may be looking for." He laughed at my continued attempt to find them. "There are no beams or anything. Besides, you fell asleep whenever we passed through one."

"I did?" That explained my constant dips into unconsciousness.

"Yes, when a person isn't accustomed to it, repeated passes take a lot of energy from them. It's a pain in the ass, but it comes in handy when dealing with the occasional human that stumbles across one that is carelessly left open. Most of the time they can't remember what happened, and those who do require very little persuasion to change their minds."

He grabbed our bags from the trunk and transferred them to a different vehicle; a large truck that he said would be able to handle the terrain better. I tried to help, but he didn't allow me to do much. I stopped trying to figure out where we were going or how we were getting there. After the whole portal discussion, it felt useless to even try. One day I would understand it all, I hoped.

We drove through the dark empty land faster than I thought we should have. It felt like we would never see light again outside of the two beams that highlighted the road ahead. The blackness that wrapped around the truck made me sick; it felt like more than darkness. More than once, I could have sworn the damn stuff was moving, reminding me of my dream, and I recoiled from it, tucking myself as far away from the door as I could.

The best thing I could do was look away from the window, so I decided to use Lacal's face as a calming agent. It would have worked, but he seemed too tense; the longer we drove, the worse it got. I couldn't tell if it was because of me, or if he was bothered by something else entirely. Yes, I was still insecure. I had no idea why. After all that he had told me, I should have been sure of his feelings, but I wondered; did he like me because he really liked me or did he like me because he was bonded to me?

We drove for hours before I saw any light. I refused to look at the clock knowing it would only make it worse. Off in the distance, the glow was dim at first, barely visible. As we continued, it grew wider and brighter. Eventually, the source of light was revealed, and it was 719, a small town alive with festivities. We could hear the music as we approached. He stopped the car outside the edge of town, just before we reached the ring of light.

Twenty- Five

"What's the matter? Why did you stop?" I wanted him to continue driving so that we would finally be out of the darkness.

"To warn you one last time," he put the car in park and ran his hands through his hair.

"About?" I looked behind us and let out a sigh of relief that there wasn't any movement in the darkness. Perhaps it was all in my head, nerve induced hallucinations.

"About what's going to happen once we get in there." He turned in his seat to face me. He looked normal, like himself, only nervous. Did he think I would change my mind? Was he afraid that I would disappoint him?

"And that is?" I swallowed the lump of worry that formed in my throat.

"They know you're coming, the entire town. There will be ceremonies, meetings, questions, and a constant stream of people eager to get your attention and affection. I don't know how long it will take. It may last for days, possibly weeks."

"You've already expressed all of that to me. Clearly my arrival, if I am who you think, would be a big deal. I'm okay, Lacal." I reached across the space between us and pulled his hand from his lap into my own.

"It's just… they knew the moment I laid eyes on you. That light started to grow as our bond did, and now with you approaching, it's like a beacon, letting everyone know how close to home you are. It's the tree, Rasmiyah; she is announcing your presence and welcoming you home."

"All of that light is coming from a tree?" I turned towards the light. It spread for miles outside of the town.

"Yes, think of it as something of an alarm system. You're here now and everyone knows it. It can sense the magic in your blood, and the bond between us, and it's calling to you now. Can you feel it?" He squeezed my hand.

"I don't know what I feel," I took a deep breath. "What do we do now? We're supposed to go in right? I'm assuming we can't just sit here forever."

"If you want to, I'm not going to force you. If you want to turn around and drive away, we will." He said it as a comfort for me, but I could tell it was much more for him. That was what he wanted. I had accepted this change in my life. Well, as much as I could in just three days. I never stopped to question if he had. It seemed it was now my turn to be his pillar of strength.

To know that everyone was expecting me, and they knew how close I was made it impossible for me to leave now. We had come this far and when I centered myself, I could feel something pulling me further. I couldn't turn away from it. I tightened my grip on his hand, forced a tight smile and nodded forward.

The car pulled forward, slowly approaching the village. We then passed what looked like a gateway. The entrance was made of a strange silver coated metal that was shaped into an arch and bent into intricate designs that spiraled from the top down to the ground. As we continued forward we started to pass a few buildings. They were all empty and dark. As we drove into the town we began to see buildings and homes that were lit up. The further we drove, the more elaborate the lights and decorations became.

"Is there a holiday happening?" I asked without thinking.

"What?"

"All the decorations, what are they for?"

"They are for you, Alexa," he looked at me and smiled, it should have been obvious.

"Me? Why? That's a little more than I was prepared for." I hadn't expected all the fanfare. I'm not sure what I did expect, but this felt like too much. I could have smacked myself in the head for being so absent minded. What if I didn't pass the test? It all seemed a little premature.

"I tried to warn you. You are the *queen* Alexa. Of course, there has to be fanfare." He chuckled. I liked the sound of him laughing; even if it was at my expense.

"Promise you won't leave me?" I tightened my hold on his hand which was still wrapped inside my own and he gave me a squeeze back and smiled at me. The wave a nausea hit me the closer we got to that beacon of light. It didn't help that that word was there again. Queen. I was no queen. I thought about asking him to turn around and take me back home where I was just a regular girl who hated shopping and ran track.

"Never." The word seemed to answer both questions. The one I had asked and the one I hadn't.

When we arrived at the center of town, it wasn't quite the ambush I was expecting. We got out of the car and everyone was gathered around all dressed up in their 'Sunday's best'. The women wore long dresses with elaborate designs of lace and silk. The men were all in suits, even the little boys. No one approached us. They remained at a distance, staring and whispering in hushed tones.

"I feel underdressed," I only meant to think it, but the words slipped through my lips, a strained whisper.

"What?"

"I thought you said they were going to attack." I looked around at the crowd and in seconds became stunned with paranoia.

"They will, but not yet." He led me away from the car, I followed close behind.

"What are they waiting for?" I whispered.

"I told you, Rasmiyah has to except you, embrace us and forge the bond, sealing it and unlocking your powers." He stared straight ahead. His level of nervousness matched my own.

"And, that's supposed to happen now?"

"Yes, is that a problem?" He stopped walking and turned to me.

"I don't know, I thought there would be some more time. Maybe a special dinner and ceremony or something before all of this happened." I was panicking, and he could feel it.

"No one else is allowed in and no one will approach you until they know for sure that you are the High Arc." He smiled sympathetically.

"And, how will they know that?" Was I going to be getting a tattoo? Did I have to be branded with a symbol to let everyone know who I was?

"You'll be alive," he turned from me and started walking again. I hurried to catch up, pulled him to a stop and forced him to look at me.

"Alive, you mean as in not dead? Why would I not be alive, Lacal?" I whispered to him in tiny panicked screeches, trying not to show the crowd of onlookers the fear that had sprung up into my throat and was now trying to choke the life from me.

"The process would most likely kill you if you weren't the one. On the off chance that you survived that there are people who would feel that you know too much about our people and our culture to let you live."

"Okay, wait. That's kind of harsh. Couldn't they just erase my memory or something and portal wave me back to my house?" My eyes darted across the crowd. Which one in this sea of seemingly kind faces would be the one to strike the fatal blow? My legs twitched as I thought of running for the car. How many could I outrun, and if I did manage to make it out of the town, where the hell would I go? I would freeze to death in the creepy darkness that waited outside the town line.

"Alexa, don't worry. You're the High Arc. We both know that," He made sure our eyes met as he challenged me. He was right. I could feel it in me, but that feeling, that power surge, it didn't erase the death threat I had just received.

"You may already know this, hell I'm sure you do, but I have to say, a small part of me is starting to second guess this whole thing. You know, now that my death is on the table," I gave him the toughest look I could master and waited to see if he was developing any doubts like I was, but he still looked the same. I was the one he had spent years searching for and nothing would change that for him.

241

"Don't worry, okay," he grabbed my hand again and led me through the entrance of the temple. I gulped as I headed to the tree, the spirit, and possibly my death.

Twenty- Six

The temple was exactly as he had described it. The entire inside was an elaborate extension of the tree. The roots shot up from the ground below it and into the air forming a frozen fortress of limbs and leaves. The outside, the brick layers around it had been constructed by the people in the town to protect what lived inside. It smelled of nothing but earth. Entirely lit by the light emanating from the tree, the room glowed so brightly that I had to squint and wait for my eyes to adjust to the light.

Lacal tightened his grip on my hand sensing my growing apprehension to continue. At the point of contact, I could feel energy moving from him into me. As his vitality raced across my body, it dissolved the block between me and Rasmiyah. I could feel her. She called to me. I smiled as I looked to the center of the room and saw the Weeping Willow.

My heart skipped a beat, it was a sign. My love for the Willow had to have been because of her. The tree felt more alive than anything I had ever encountered before. I could now see it for what it was; it was much more than a tree. It was Rasmiyah, and connected to a part of me. There was movement in the walls. I looked closer to find that they were not frozen, but moving, breathing, feeding the tree; and calling to my soul.

There was a song. I could hear it, barely, coming from the heart of the tree. Airy tones, what I would assume angels sounded like, called out to me and beckoned me to join them, and, I wanted to. Every cell in my body began to call back to them, joining in their song, and rejoicing my return to what was undoubtedly my home.

I stepped forward. The tables turned. It was now I who towed Lacal with me. I had to be with them, the melodic voices in my head. I couldn't wait any longer. Every step I took brought another pulse of energy. The light of the tree moved with those pulses, traveling into my body and warming me to my core. It felt warm and freeing and purifying.

As we reached the center of the room and the base of the tree, I looked down at my hands and I saw the light underneath my skin. It moved and danced throughout my limbs, and I embraced it. I turned to Lacal and saw that he looked the same as I did. He looked first at himself and then at me and smiled.

"You look so beautiful." He touched my face and held his hand there. I leaned into him and covered his hand with mine.

"Is this how it felt the first time you were here? This is amazing, I feel so good. I can't even find the words to express it." I smiled at him and wanted to kiss him.

"No, this is new. See, I told you, you're the one, Alexa. All of this wouldn't be happening if you weren't." He looked at me like a kid preparing to open the largest gift under the Christmas tree.

"Yeah, you were right, about everything," I stepped closer to him pressing my body up against his.

"So, are you ready for this?" He asked me and turned away to look at the tree.

"I don't know exactly what 'this' is, but yes I'm ready." I turned to face the tree as well. Our hands fell from my face, but we didn't lose contact. We laced our fingers together.

He placed his free hand on the trunk then motioned for me to do the same. I did, placing my hand right next to his. I felt a prick in the palm of my hand, a tiny point of pain followed by an overpowering sense of euphoria.

The energy from the tree poured into us, and the glow beneath our skin intensified until we were lit up almost as bright as the Willow itself. The voices, once singing, were now sighing with contentment as the branches reached around us, tying together and sealing us in our own cocoon away from the world.

I assumed it would be over. It was exactly what Lacal had described, a cocoon and light. We stood there, looking at each other and nothing happened. I wanted to speak, but I couldn't ruin the moment with words. There really were no words to say.

A few seconds passed before the dance of lights began. The leaves of the tree broke away from the limbs and floated around us, flickering green and gold. They covered us from head to toe. When the last leaf touched my skin, I felt as if I was being ripped from my body.

Lacal had the same experience, it was painless, but it shocked him just as much as it did me. We were floating above ourselves. I cannot describe my appearance, but Lacal appeared as a shadowy form of himself. He was no more than a show of light. His features were his own, only faded and transparent. I stared down in disbelief at my body frozen solid and covered completely in the glowing leaves. We looked like a pair of statues, long forgotten monuments overrun by nature.

I tried to tell him how amazing and completely unnerving it all was, but I couldn't. Not because I was afraid of ruining the moment, or because I could not find the words. When I opened my mouth, no sound came out. Like someone had flipped the off switch on my voice box and denied me the ability to speak.

Once again, we were waiting. We floated there, and I felt like there was something we were supposed to be doing to make the process continue. I listened to my instincts and floated over to him. Don't ask me how, I just wished I could hold his hand again. Next thing I knew, I was closing in on his translucent figure.

REVITALIZED

The expression on his face told how uncomfortable he felt. It was strange how natural it felt to me. It was obviously not the same for him. While I had an easy understanding of it, he wasn't sure how to handle what was happening. I reached out for him and pulled him to me. Nothing happened. I gingerly wrapped my arms around him, when they didn't go through him like I thought they would, I pulled him closer to me and kissed him.

We were pressed together. An outside force, like one of the strongest winds that Chicago could produce, wrapped around us and blended us together. The pressure was crushing, but his kiss made it bearable. I opened my eyes and watched as his lids fluttered open as well.

I could see them, my grey orbs of comfort watching me before exploding into beams of fire. The light shot from his eyes into mine and then returned. We were being melded together, two beings turned into one. Our very essences were tied together, and it felt amazing.

The light stopped, and I gasped for air, even though in this state, I had no need to breathe. I hadn't been breathing the entire time. He looked at me and kissed me again. I'm not sure if it was necessary, but it felt amazing. Better than all the kisses before it. There was a new level of closeness, a feeling of utter unity.

The outside force loosened its grip slowly and then disappeared altogether. I kept my arms around him, not ready to let him go. This experience was too good to give up so easily. We stayed that way for a few moments, but that inner urge told me I needed to let go. As I released my grip from around his neck, I heard a voice in my head.

It sounded almost like my grandmother, but the tone was much deeper, older. I looked to Lacal with a questioning gaze. Could he hear it as well? He nodded and pointed at the heart of the tree.

"Welcome home Alexa. I am elated to see that you have decided to take your rightful place as High Arc. You are now forever bonded with your Serve and all of the High Arcs before you. On your soul has been forged a piece of his and on his, a piece of yours. It appears there is a lot for you to learn. This will be a setback for you. I am afraid there isn't very much time." Her voice turned somber. Erasing the feeling of euphoria and replacing it with fear. "You must train and prepare yourself. Danger is coming, Alexa. It is now your duty to protect our people and all the people of this world from the darkness that threatens it.

Use your Serve, he will help you, protect you, and guide you; but it is up to you to fight this battle. No one else is capable. You have been chosen by blood, by heritage. I know the strength is in you. You have faced much heart ache and managed to survive and grow stronger because of it. I admit the level of difficulty will be much greater, but I am confident that you can handle it. Your soul is the strongest a High Arc has had in many eons, and your Serve the most loyal I have seen. Use this to your advantage.

Darkness thrives on destruction. It will stop at nothing to break you, everything, and everyone in your life that gives you strength. Don't allow it to destroy you or your bond. It may not seem so now, but you are not alone in this. Your friends and family will be by your side, but trust me when I tell you, that alone will not help you win this war.

Pull strength from them. Open yourself up to the help and guidance they have to offer to you. Inside of you lives the essence of me and all your mothers and we are here for you when you need us," the voice stopped, and we were shot back into our bodies.

The leaves fell off and slid over the ground back up to their places the tree. The branches unwrapped themselves from around us. I opened my eyes and I felt different. I felt stronger, her words were true. I could feel Lacal, or at least a part of him, inside of me now. The amazing sensation this brought me wasn't one that I was able to stop and enjoy. All I could think about was the warning I had received.

"Wait!" I screamed at the tree and looked at Lacal. "What was that, danger, save the world?"

"I don't know." There was something, a flicker in our bond. A nudge that told me he was hiding something.

"So, you're telling me that you didn't get that message the first time around?" I did not want to accuse

249

him of any wrong doing but I felt like I had been tricked into doing something that I had no business taking part in.

"No," he looked shocked, "I told you what happened. There was just that strong urge, the impulse to get to you. I had to bring you home."

"I cannot believe this! Is this why all the other High Arcs didn't accept?" I pointed my finger at the tree accusingly. It wasn't Lacal who had tricked me. It was Rasmiyah and that thing, that instinct that said it was okay to come to her. It told me the right thing to do was to accept this unacceptable change in my life. "Did the others know about this 'war' before they were forced into taking on the responsibility of an entire planet?!"

"Alexa, no," he was leaving something out, but at this point I did not care what it was, I wanted to find a way out of having to carry the weight of the world on my shoulder. That is exactly what it was. The World. The entire planet was now depending on me to protect it.

"What am I supposed to do now? I can't handle this, Lacal. I know my life hasn't been the easiest but, this is just too much." My nerves were rattled, and my limbs trembled. He grabbed me by the shoulders, pulled me into his arms, and kissed my forehead. My moment of strength had ended.

"This is a lot. I know it is. You will be okay Alexa. Let's go find my father; he will know what to do." I doubted that his father could be of any real help.

Unless he had a quick fix for the damnation of the world, I was screwed. I followed him anyway; eager to get away from this tree and forget the message it had given me.

To avoid the crowd, we exited through a door in the back floor. I could hear the murmurs, the excitement. They all knew I was the real deal now. Lacal feared that they would be led to think otherwise. If I appeared looking so distraught it would cause them to worry. He was sure they wouldn't jump to harming me. Some might look at it as finishing the job that Rasmiyah left incomplete. I should not survive if I were not queen. He was sure this wouldn't happen, but he didn't want to take any chances.

I agreed with his decision. Even if I was capable of lying, I would never be able to put on a good enough show to satisfy their expectations of their new High Arc. Not after hearing that all of their lives were on the line and I was responsible for defending them.

Twenty-Seven

It had been months of practicing, grueling days and nights simply trying to learn the basics. Not universe splitting material, but calming, centering, aura reading crap. I was beyond frustrated with the level of difficulty. The passage of power wasn't as simple as Lacal, his father, or that damn tree made it sound. I hadn't been back there. Of course, it was pointed out to me, the benefits of choosing to return. The knowledge I could only receive while inside the temple; but, I felt betrayed. Every time I felt close to going back, I would remember that feeling. Yes, it was a foolish decision on my part, but I didn't care.

The day after my arrival, I was put through the awakening process. Lacal's father performed the ceremony. I refused to do it at the temple, so we did it inside the Town Hall which sat directly across the town's center from the temple. The process was simple enough. I lay on a table and was given some green gook to drink. An old lady came in and started saying a prayer in the original language. The only time I understood her was when she said my name.

REVITALIZED

I could feel the thick fluid as it moved inside of me. It absorbed itself into my bloodstream and used my own adrenaline to aid in its journey to my heart. I felt its slimy touch enter my chest cavity and then I passed out. When I woke up, I felt different. I was expecting to be an animal, but I wasn't.

The world felt different...new. The air, it burned my lungs and left funny tastes in my mouth. Everything smelled disgusting. Even the flowers across the room, their fragrance was much too strong. I wrinkled my nose as I sat up. Everything was as I was told it would be. My movements seemed too fast, my eyesight too sharp. I gripped the side of the bed and my fingers left their imprint in the metal frame. It took a while to get myself adjusted, but not as long as I had feared it would. On the table beside, me were three glasses filled with different liquids, orange, white and red. One looked like orange soda, one had to be milk or yogurt, and the other I could only assume by its thick consistency was blood. I knew I should have gone for the blood. The reason for this process was to make me a full vampire, but I just had to know what regular foods tasted like. Lacal would never tell me.

I picked the glass of orange soda and gulped it down and sat it back on the table. It tasted the same, only less impressive, that was disappointing. Heightened taste buds were not fooled by artificial sweeteners. The smell was off, sweeter than I remembered, but, that was the only real change. Before I could attempt to grab the glass of milk to sample it, I doubled over and cleared my stomach of its orange contents. Were it not for the lack of blood or body matter I would have sworn all of my insides had been ripped out of me and thrown to the floor. Lacal rushed in and helped me to a chair. He held back a smile as he handed me the glass of blood.

"Sorry, we all have to learn the lesson."

"Lesson, what lesson?" I wiped my mouth with the back of my hand hoping there weren't any puke chunks. "I saw you eating Lacal, at our picnic, and at my house. You didn't have any reaction to it."

"You haven't had any blood. Your body cannot process anything unless it has what it truly needs. Eating human foods is something we do to fit in, besides, some of it actually tastes pretty good; but if we don't listen to our instincts and keep ourselves properly nourished with blood, we will get sick and eventually die."

"It would have been nice to know that before." I punched him in the shoulder and swallowed the rest of the blood.

The taste was too good for description. Imagine drinking sunshine coated in honey and dipped in chocolate. It energized me. Everything intensified. The sights, sounds, and smells, what I thought was astonishing before became so much more. The increase of my sensory perception was also accompanied by an increase of my thirst. I craved more. I looked to Lacal who understood and quickly produced another glass.

When I finished that one, he refused my quest for a third. I was told I had to learn to tame my thirst and not let it overpower me. Losing control meant turning to Darkness, and that wasn't an option. He thought it was a good idea to start that lesson plan right away.

Great, just add that to the challenge of mastering all of my untold gifts. No sweat! I thought of my problem, of how I could not figure out what gifts I was supposed to have. When I did figure one out, I then had to learn how to control it. Manipulations over the physical world and moving things around with my mind, was something I excelled at. I barely even tried, they were like natural reactions, but everything else was much more complicated, even more so without someone to train me.

I learned mostly from the few random historic writings I lucked out in finding. They gave partial descriptions of some of the gifts of a High Arc, but never had any indication of how she managed to use them. So of course, this left me frustrated and staring at dead ends. It was the worst feeling, to know I had the ability to perform such miraculous things and yet not be able to figure out how to make it happen.

I wished the previous High Arc, whoever she was, would show her ass up, and help me figure it all out. Didn't she feel some sort of need or responsibility to help me? That unfortunately, never happened and I gave up on hoping that it would. I was on my own, which sad to say, was something I had become accustomed to.

Lacal tried to help, but was only a tad bit more than completely useless. However, he made an awesome test dummy. His dad Lamar was able to provide me with some useful guidance. He knew all about the simpler powers and how to unlock them. He also knew the rules and basic properties of controlling any power. Whenever I needed to test a new theory of power, Lacal stood in. Lamar said that my fear of harming him would aid me in my control.

I was told that Layal would have been more help. She was one of the few people around who studied the old traditions and practiced their lessons faithfully. She had been taught by her mother. Unfortunately for me, when we arrived we found out that Layal had decided to leave 719. She gave no reason for her decision, nor did she make any promises to return. All she said was that a change was coming, and everyone had to choose what side they were on and fight for that side. Apparently, she'd chosen her side and it didn't look like that side was ours.

After we told him about the message that was given to us, Lamar decided that it was best not to tell the community about it. I was surprised to find out how many people had already suspected something was wrong though they were all vague in their reasoning for their suspicions. Most just claimed it was something they could sense in the air. They might not have been completely sure what was coming, but they knew it was something bad and something powerful. Yay me!

The younger crowd sometimes questioned why I wasn't out and about more. They thought that I should have been out mingling with them. Instead I spent most of my time in training. They did very little speculating. Eventually they all became bored, downright uninterested in the subject.

I met everyone in the town in the first few days before diving into practice. They all brought gifts and offerings and praised me for choosing to come. This would have been a great experience had I not been trying to find a way to escape. Each time I gave a plastic smile and tried to accept it all as graciously as I could manage. To know that a tour of sorts was coming didn't help. It would be expected of me to visit other villages and meet literally every person.

It helped that from most of the people, I felt genuine love and appreciation. It made it easier to get through the lineup. However, there were the occasional spiteful smiles masking total disgust. These were the individuals who made going back to my old life look like fun. I would have jumped at the chance not to have to be bothered with people who didn't even want me around to begin with. If they didn't want me there, I could leave. I could pass the crown on to the next girl in line.

The last person I met was Jemal, Lacal's ex-best friend. He had apparently waited outside and then pounced on his chance to be alone with me when Lacal had been called away. Truly my Serve, he rarely left my side as he promised he would, but sometimes it was necessary. I wasn't the only one with an ever-growing list of things to do. I felt sorry for Lacal, always trying to be supportive to me. Who would support him?

I sensed Jemal before he approached. His presence made my stomach turn. I looked up to find him watching me from the entrance to the hall. He walked towards me and I wished I had taken Lacal up on his offer to join him when he left to see his father. Now I was alone, and I had no idea what this stranger was planning to do.

Twenty- Eight

"My queen." He handed me a basket of fruits, which I accepted, but had no intention of eating. He then performed an overly exaggerated and totally unnecessary bow.

"Hi," I smiled at him, because it was expected of me.

"Welcome to our humble little village, my name is Jemal." He held his hand out to me.

"Oh," I paused not knowing how to continue, I had suspected it was him, but hadn't been prepared to speak to him.

It was then that he began to stand out from the swarm of the faces I had seen throughout the day. He was someone to remember and not just because he was last in line. I'm not sure why I noticed so much about him or why I took the time to catalog him in my mind. I blamed it on my newly heightened vampire senses and ignored the fact that I hadn't done it with anyone else. I told myself it was because he was alone, there were no distractions.

He was tall, taller than Lacal. His hair was short and dark, cut down like he had just enlisted in the military. I guess he did it because he thought it went well with his position as head of security. His skin was like Lacal's, that same clear complexion, slightly milky, only tanner; he must have enjoyed sun bathing.

He wore tight jeans and black turtle neck shirt that seemed too tight. It hugged his skin and bragged to the world how he kept his body fit. It was obvious that he had planned it that way. He wanted me to see what I was missing out on. Too bad for him, muscles were not my thing. Some guys just overdid it; they became more muscle than man. Jemal was nearly one of them.

"I take it you've heard about me." He grinned wide showing every tooth in his smug head. He was so full of himself, it was sickening.

"Briefly, yes," I tensed. He didn't particularly like Lacal, and that alone had caused me to become defensive.

"Hmm," he rolled his eyes.

"What?"

"I would have thought I was worth more than a brief mentioning, considering the fact that I was the one meant to be by your side." He crossed his arms resembling a pouting child.

"Calling it a fact seems just a tad inaccurate don't you think?" I smiled and tilted my head at him, mocking his dramatic show.

"How so?" He sounded like I had actually offended him by correcting his statement.

"If you were meant for me, you would have been chosen, but you were not, were you? As it was told to me, Rasmiyah rejected you but she did not reject Lacal." Pride resonated in my voice as I said it. I loved Lacal and I didn't appreciate anyone trying to put him down in my presence, especially not Jemal.

"Yeah, well he is crap and in no time his gooey little spine will have you wishing it was me by your side." He pounded his chest with his fist in the most juvenile display of bravado I had ever seen. "A real man."

"Right now, I can tell you honestly that I doubt that will ever happen." His apelike display caused me to laugh a bit.

"You bitch!" He reached for me, but, was sent flying backwards and into the wall. I hadn't seen him come in and apparently neither had Jemal, but Lacal was now in front of me. His body was half crouched with his back towards me; ready for an attack. There was something there, watching him ready to protect me. I felt complete exhilaration. He was fierce, sexy. I told myself that this was not the time.

"I believe you meant to say, your highness!" Lacal yelled at Jemal who simply whimpered.

He had knocked Jemal clear across the room. Jemal looked completely dumbfounded. He stared at his once best friend, unable to believe what had just happened. He huffed and struggled to pull himself upright, then stumbled out of the room cursing the both of us. The only thing left of him was the impression of his back in the wall. Lamar would not like that one bit.

"What was that?" I got up from my seat and went to Lacal's side.

"I don't know," he looked down at his hands. "I'm sorry."

"No! Don't be! That was totally bad ass!" I grabbed his arm and smiled at him. He smiled back, kissed my forehead and escorted me to my next training session.

I hadn't seen Jemal after that, and I didn't have a need to. He was obviously out of his mind. To allow myself to be anywhere near him would be a bad idea. There was no doubt that he would try to hurt me again if ever given the chance.

My exercise for the night had been cut short. Lamar thought it was important for me to take a break. He said I had been working too much. Over training would lead to making careless and costly mistakes. I didn't know if I agreed, but I was happy for the reprieve.

There was a festival happening in the center of town. It was in celebration of the anniversary of the founding of the village. My history lessons taught me that over the last 700 years it had outgrown the right to be classified as a village. It annoyed me, for whatever reason I do not know. The population alone was too much, but that was still what everyone seemed to prefer to call it. Lamar insisted that it kept them humble and peaceful. They had no real problems, outside of the few town drunks, but really, no place big or small would be complete without them.

I was surprised to find the founder there when I arrived. She didn't live in town, and before meeting her, I was skeptical that she was still alive. She sat at the long table to the left of my seat, which was in the center. We sat at the head of the festivities, right outside of the Arc temple. The one place I didn't want to be, and yet every major event was held here. I turned to my right to find Lacal, in the same place he always sat. He stood and pulled my chair out for me.

I stared at the founder, Reniah. For someone who was over 700 years old, she looked fantastic. She appeared to be only in her early 40's. She moved like my grandmother, graceful. Every movement was deliberate and controlled. I couldn't watch her and not compare the two.

It was easier not to think of my grandmother. I was still unable to understand why she left the way she did. She had to have known what I was walking into. She provided a cure to my disease only to make sure that I did so. The worse part about it all was that no one knew her. I asked around. I targeted every elder in the village. They couldn't provide me with any explanation for why she did what she did. I had zero hope that she would be showing up to apologize.

The festival was exactly what I had come to expect. No freaky vampire rituals or traditions. There weren't any sacrifices of humans. It was all normal and it made me sick to my stomach because it wasn't normal at all. There were parades, dancing and singing; followed by food and then more drunken dancing. It was all very human, and it didn't fit.

I sat in front of the High Arc temple with the founder and Lacal. There wasn't much comfort in being at the forefront of every event, but it was getting easier to swallow. Few people paid any attention to me. I was just another feature now, another decoration for the party. It would be no different if I were not there.

To be honest, being the High Arc hadn't been that difficult outside of the physical and mental training. I wasn't asked to make any major decisions or attend any boring Council meetings. My responsibilities were studying, training, and making appearances at events when necessary. Lamar told me when I was ready to step up and take on full responsibility it would be my right to. Until then, no one would try to force me to do so. I made no complaints, not one peep.

"You look bored," Lacal bumped my shoulder with his.

"Is it that obvious? I'd rather be training now." I sighed. He smiled, and as always, I melted.

"You need to take a break. You have been going non-stop for weeks." He took a sip from his cup; from the smell I could tell it was blood. It didn't really bother me as much as I thought it would. My mind was preoccupied with mulling over more important things, like saving the world from dangers unknown.

"You know why I have been training so hard," I rolled my eyes at him. The music was loud, so it was unnecessary to whisper like we usually would.

"Yes I do. But I also know that if you're not rested, all the training you're doing won't matter." He put his hand on my shoulder, but I shrugged it off. I could feel how much this hurt him, but it was causing me more irritation than comfort.

"Well, I guess I will have to deal with that when it's necessary." I snapped at him, my frustration was because I knew what he said was true. Unfortunately for me, there weren't many other options.

"And it will be Alexa." He pushed further.

"Drop it please," I snapped at him. My temper had become an issue. I had been able to control my thirst. But something else happened. Something I was never warned about. Slowly in the days after, I began to think and feel dark things. I was more temperamental than I had ever been, snapping at people for simply trying to help me. I put myself in isolation because of this but I told no one, I couldn't. I was afraid of what the people would think. I was afraid of what Lacal would think. The broken Serve and his defective High Arc.

Of course, I was told by so many people that this was because of lack of rest. How could I rest knowing there was pure evil headed towards Earth, and it was on my shoulders to go up against it? Regardless of all that they said, I knew that it had nothing to do with rest or lack thereof. The change I felt, it was deeper, and it was real. Sleep would not chase the demons away. They were a part of me now, and they were here to stay, I knew it. I just didn't know what it meant for me, or the people I was meant to protect.

Twenty- Nine

I watched as the people, my people, enjoyed themselves. Each of them was oblivious to the approaching danger. I was envious of their ignorance. I wished I could just dance and sing, and not be concerned about anything but where my next drink was coming from. That was no longer possible for me.

Two hours past and we sat in silence. I didn't feel like talking, which thankfully wasn't hard to achieve considering that the founder was, more or less, a zombie throughout the entire event. She barely spoke to me when I sat down, and seemed truly annoyed by having to be there. Once, I thought I heard her mumble something about heathens, but I really wasn't paying much attention. Our lack of interest in the event was equaled.

The night began to weigh on me. I was tired, mind and body. Sitting in the middle of a party having music blasted at every angle of my head was not helping me relax. The celebration was still going strong and didn't look to be ending any time soon.

"I think I'm going to call it a night," I pushed my chair back from the table. This caused the legs to scrape the ground, and earned me a very dirty look from the founder.

"Okay, I'll walk you home." Lacal started to get up but I placed my arm on his shoulder stopping him. I loved his company and looked forward to it most days, but I needed space. I needed some time to myself.

"No, stay, enjoy yourself. You have been babysitting me long enough." He didn't argue, and I was happy for that. Yet I was irritated that he didn't contest to my calling it, babysitting.

I decided to go home. The streets were clear. Everyone was in the center of town. This gave me time to absorb the scenery, something I hadn't had much chance to do. Usually I was rushing from one location to the next trying to avoid the crowds.

It was all cobble stone streets and buildings made of bricks. Very few updates were made to the buildings close to the center of town. I imagined they looked almost exactly the same as when they were first built. The ground was covered in snow and I should have been freezing, but I barely felt a chill.

Since my Awakening, my body temperature ran about 10 degrees hotter. This of course went against common theory. Vampires were supposed to be ice boxes. The thin jacket I wore was actually beginning to cause me to sweat. I was told this effect was caused by my body reacting to the change. It would eventually wear off, and I would cool down to well below normal temperature. Yet, even after I cooled down, my skin would never feel like ice.

The house was the last on the street. Lacal's childhood home. The lights were on inside and the door was open allowing the yellow beams of light to spill out onto the street. Something wasn't right. Everyone was still at the celebration. I walked to the door cautiously, trying not to get my heart rate up and alert Lacal. I didn't want him to come running if there was nothing really out of sorts.

"Lamar?" I peered around the corner of the door hoping he would shout out from the kitchen. It would be great if he were cooking, I could really use some food, and I hadn't eaten a thing at the festival. My griping stomach would have to wait. Lamar was not home, but the house was not unoccupied.

Two girls who looked to be about 17 years old, stood in the middle of the hall. They were identical twins. To emphasize the obvious, they wore matching snow suits, one pink and one purple. They had deep caramel complexions and large round hazel eyes. They were average height and very slim. The one in the pink had pig tails, and the one in purple had braids. She was curvier than her sister. Both of their hair fell past their shoulders.

"Um...hi?" I stepped across the threshold into the house and left the door open behind me. I didn't want any obstacles if I needed to make a run for it. They gave me a bad feeling and the little voice inside me warned me to be cautious. I had learned to listen to that voice.

"Hi," the girl in purple said. "I'm Menaria and this is my sister Nadia," Nadia giggled and waved, Menaria rolled her eyes.

"I'm Alexa," I said stepping forward with my hand held out to shake. Perhaps they were friends of Lacal's coming to visit. My hand hung in front of me. Neither of them took it.

"We know who you are," Nadia giggled. It was supposed to sound innocent, but fell horribly short. The sinister sound clashed with her wholesome look.

"Okay?" I stepped back, closer to the door. I was beginning to panic; I tried to remind myself not to. I had to remain calm.

"We have a message for you," Nadia said with more giggling, this time accompanied by a theatrical bow.

"Get over the antics Nadia; I don't want to be here all night," Menaria tossed her braids over her shoulder and crossed her arms over her chest.

"A message...from who?" I looked from Nadia to Menaria. She would give me the answers without the show.

"Jocelyn," Menaria huffed.

270

"And who is Jocelyn?" Perhaps I should have known that name, but I didn't.

"He didn't tell you?" Nadia giggled again which was seriously starting to get on my nerves. She was fiddling with a folded piece of paper.

"Lacal can clarify that," Menaria snatched the piece of paper from Nadia and handed it to me. She clearly didn't want to be there, I wondered if she was being forced.

I unfolded and read the note.

Alexa,
Hey bitch.
I have your friend. You want her? Come get her.
-Jocelyn
P.S.
Love my new shiny red Porsche!

"What is this?" I held the paper out towards them.

"You read it, I'm sure you understood it, it's not that difficult to decipher. Our job was to deliver the message and that's done," Menaria said as they pushed past me and moved for the exit. "Oh, and you have three days to comply. Trust me; she isn't the patient kind, she won't hesitate to kill her."

"Excuse me?" I could feel my blood begin to boil.

271

"Look I'm the messenger there is your message. Bye." Menaria pushed past me, Nadia followed.

"You think you can just come in here, threaten me, and just leave?"

Nadia turned, smiled and said simply. "Yes."

"Like hell!" The anger, the temper that I had been trying to subdue, it all boiled to the top. The world began to shake around me. The floor rocked, and the two girls fought to maintain their balance. "You aren't going anywhere!" I yelled.

Menaria moved towards me, she was quick, but I was quicker. Her body flew backwards, slammed into the door frame and knocked it off of its hinges. Nadia charged at me, but I used my mind to cut off her airways. She clawed at her throat trying to remove the hand that was not there. That silly little grin was missing as her complexion changed to an odd shade of blue.

"She will die!" Menaria yelled.

Those three words were enough to break my concentration. That's all it took, Lamar had warned me. One instance of weakness and your opponent will take you down. The room started to spin, and I felt a pressure so strong on the inside of my head that I actually feared it would cause my brain to explode.

The grip I had on Nadia failed. As she got to her feet, my vision blurred, and my chest tightened, refusing to let air into my lungs. I spun around trying to find my bearings. Nadia and Menaria were standing in the doorway again. Their blurry figures seemed to tower over me. I tried to remain alert but my oxygen deprived brain was fading quickly.

I could see their eyes. They were wide and glazed over, but, I could tell they were focusing on me. Whatever this pain was that I was feeling inside of my head was there because they put it there.

I heard Nadia's giggles ringing inside my head like bells and then I was on the floor. My body curled up and I crushed the note in a tight fist. The world slipped away and then popped back into focus with a painful sharpness. I was back in my grandmother's empty house. The lack of her presence screamed at me. She was gone. She hated me. She was gone. My vision flooded with tears and I completely shut down.

"Alexa? Alexa, can you hear me?" I heard his frightened voice, but, I couldn't find him. I tried to move towards his voice and let him save me from this, but I couldn't. I was trapped.

Then I saw her face, floating above me, red hair matted with dirt. Tears streamed down her face, she was out of reach. I fought to get to her, but every step I took forward only sent her further away from me. She was scared and alone and if I didn't do something to stop them, she would die. There was no way I could let that happen to Jazz. Not after all that she had done for me.

I pulled away from the darkness and away from my friend. I struggled against its tight grip and towed my heavy form towards Lacal's voice. It was hard to turn away but following Jazz's image was only sending her deeper into the darkness and taking me further away from any chance of actually saving her.

I opened my eyes to find his distraught face hovering above my own. I reached up and touched his cheek. I had to make sure he was real and wouldn't move away like Jazz had. He smiled, relieved that I had finally responded. He kissed my forehead and pulled me into his arms. When he released me he asked if I was okay. He asked what had happened, why the house was destroyed. I did not respond. I had my own questions to ask.

My throat burned as I spoke. But I had to get the words out. I simply had to know. "Who the hell is Jocelyn?"

About The Author

International award winning, and USA Today Bestselling author, Jessica Cage was born and raised in Chicago, IL. Growing up Jessica lived in the pages of epic fantasy books but always hoped to see herself represented in the stories. With the hope of inspiring her son to follow his dreams, Jessica picked up the pen and begin to write the stories she always wanted to star in. Now, Jessica writes characters of color in fantasy and looks forward to continuing to deliver her signature Caged Fantasies stories to readers everywhere.

JESSICA CAGE

Check out the rest of the High Arc Series:

Guidance of Rasmiyah, book 2

After finding out that she is the new Vampire Queen and that Darkness is approaching to destroy all that she loves, it is up to Alexa to fight and prove that she is ready to step up and protect her people. Jocelyn aims to steal the crown from her and will stop at nothing as she believes it is her birthright to be Queen.

Alexa is battling her own inner demon which causes her to doubt herself. Through her bond with Rasmiyah and the spirits of the previous queens, Alexa will find her strength, but she must do it quickly. Jocelyn has taken her best friend and Darkness is threatening to attack.

Alexa's Adytum, book 3

The queen is trapped inside her own mind, her Serve has been captured by Darkness, and the Navare are launching an attack in just a matter of days.

Lamar and Layal must lead the vampire masses in a battle against evil. It won't be an easy task. The Navare are nasty beasts, vampires given in to the call of Darkness. They have strength in numbers, a leader who is spiritually connected to their once queen Alecia, and a ton of twisted demons on their side.

For the vampires, its either find a way to wake Alexa or stand and fight. Which path should they choose when either may lead to their demise?

Jocelyn's Story, A High Arc Novella

REVITALIZED

Jocelyn was deemed the villain set out to take the crown from Alexa, the new Queen of their people. She was out for power, for strength and she would stop at nothing to get it. Her ambitions hurt the people around her including her own sisters and left a trail of devastation in her wake. In the end Jocelyn is taken down, but what caused her to become the person she was? What happened to his girl to make her so vengeful?